THE MORGUE KEEPER

ALSO BY RUYAN MENG

Only the Cat Knows: A Novella

THE MORGUE KEEPER

by

Ruyan Meng

7.13 Books

Printed in the United States of America

First paperback edition published by 7.13 Books, October 2025

Cover design by Olivia Croom Hammerman

www.713books.com

Speak will I of the other things I saw there.
I cannot well repeat how there I entered.
 — Dante Alighieri, *Inferno*

For my father

THE MORGUE KEEPER

1.

Thirty-seven, Qing Yuan thought when a cleaner wheeled the corpse of a woman into the morgue. The woman's husband, a scrawny man in a shabby work uniform, smelling of sewage, drooped behind the gurney. The cleaner pushed a form to Qing Yuan and fled. He glanced at it: *Dystocia with stillborn boy*.

The morgue was windowless, with just two low-wattage bulbs on the ceiling. The air lay heavy with antiseptic, cigarette smoke, rotting flesh, and blood. He looked at his watch—5:30 a.m. Another thirty minutes, he thought, and he'd be in the sun, breathing the morning air.

The husband stood numbly by, watching Qing Yuan complete the form, then shuffled out to squat against the wall to smoke. After a time Qing Yuan called him back and asked for his signature. The man scribbled what looked to Qing Yuan like a chicken's clawprint in the sand.

He filled a bowl with water and placed it on a bench near the gurney. The woman was naked under her bloody sheet. Her hair was tucked behind her ears. Her purplish hands remained clenched on her chest. She could have still been cradling her baby, Qing Yuan thought. Her pale face with its vague smile expressed neither suffering nor struggle. But as he drew back her sheet, he was sure he heard her whisper. *I have tried. I have tried so hard.*

The husband paced about, perplexed as he studied the numbered cabinets. Qing Yuan knew what the man was looking for—names. He would find none, of course, in this morgue or any other. These cabinets held nothing but nameless rotting bodies.

Qing Yuan started to clean the corpse. "Does she have any clothes?" he said.

The man fumbled in his tote, then laid a rumpled shirt, some pants, and a pair of cloth shoes on the foot of the gurney.

"Your first child?" Qing Yuan said. The man retreated to his place near the cabinets and stood there smoothing his wrinkled tote. "If you want to smoke, feel free," Qing Yuan said, and fastened a final button on the corpse's shirt.

The man glanced at the "No Smoking" sign on the wall and then at Qing Yuan. He took a cigarette from his pocket. "Want one?" he said.

Qing Yuan shook his head. He ran his fingers over the bump on the woman's belly and had the strange impression that he could sense the baby turning beneath its mother's cold skin. He wondered if a doctor or nurse had handed the baby to its mother, if she had been able to hold her baby even for a moment.

"Were you able to meet your child?" he said as he pulled the socks over the woman's swollen feet. Holes had been worn through the socks. The holes had been darned. More holes had been worn through the holes that had been darned. With a pair of dirty scissors Qin Yuan snipped the loose thread where one of the woman's toes stuck out.

"My child," the man said.

"It was a boy, yes?"

"Boy, girl, it's dead."

Government regulations stipulated that dead babies be categorized as "pathological waste" and disposed of, like garbage, in the hospital's trash bins. Qing Yuan had seen many of these tiny corpses, pinkish, yellowish, tin-gray, curled up, always seemingly asleep, tossed by janitors into fires outside the building. The scandalized

Lao Jia, the oldest morgue keeper in the hospital and Qing Yuan's one true friend—they had shared a bunk bed in a dormitory for several years—referred to the terrible act as "human incineration."

"A dead baby isn't considered a sentient being," he often complained, knowing that most of the high-ranking officials, and likely even the Supreme Leader himself, ate placenta stew, believing, ludicrously, that it would increase their masculine vitality, "and yet they reckon a placenta is worth killing for."

It was almost 6 a.m. when Qing Yuan slid the corpse into its cabinet. He left the morgue, drenched with sweat, followed by the husband, unable to make sense, Qing Yuan knew from repeated experience, of this new reality. He waved to the man as he made toward the toilet. The man stood there, his face wreathed in smoke from the cigarette between his lips.

The toilet was a narrow room, not much larger than a storage closet, lit by a sliver of light from a high tiny window. Beneath a tap connected to a rusty pipe, a concrete trough jutted from the wall, and, in the far corner, a cracked ceramic squatting pan, half-full of waste, sat on the concrete floor.

Qing Yuan opened the tap, gripped the edge of the trough, and ducked his head under the water. He stood there a long time, running his fingers through his hair, and listened to the choir of whispered sorrows that came to him every night after he had cleaned his last body. He still had to clean the morgue, he knew.

He swept the cigarette butts and ashes, the scorched matches, the dirt, the tattered bits of cloth. He paused by the mound of bloody sheets behind the door. Thirty-seven, he thought, in just eight hours, plus the child he had never seen.

He was required to clean the cabinets when needed, but he cleaned them every day just the same. He passed his rag along the doors. Now and then he paused to press his brow to a cabinet, hoping to commune with the soul inside that had refused to leave. *Most of the time I want to forget my days. Surely you all know that.* Only when he heard the echo of his voice did it strike him he'd been speaking aloud.

The air was clammy and stifling. It was always clammy and stifling. He could feel the sweat dripping from his face again. Like every day, he couldn't wait to shower. He knew he'd never be clean, of course, he'd always reek of blood and antiseptic, but every day he did his best to wash himself of these things. More than anything, he wanted to be rid of the "smack of doom" that Sister Wang, Gugu's neighbor, had said he'd stunk so foully of.

She had been a Taoist nun and, secretly, a physiognomist. Once, his aunt had invited Sister Wang to tell Qing Yuan's fortune. As Gugu sat by, Qing Yuan was told that an imbalance in his yin and yang had created too much yin qi in him. Then, to both his and Gugu's surprise, in an almost vicious undertone, Sister Wang added, "And I can see the smack of doom on your face, as well. It's everywhere," she said, and without warning ran her cold hands from Qing Yuan's brow to chin.

He swung open the locker door and glanced at his face in the small mirror Lao Jia had glued there. A gaunt pale man with gray stubble looked at him with tragic eyes. The face appalled him. That this face was his appalled him more. A shadow passed across the mirror. Someone else was with him.

There on the bare table sat Sister Wang, naked, like a crone from a tale.

"Will you clean and dress me after I die?" she said.

"I will," he said, and sat on the table. His legs dangled next to hers. She reeked of incense, as if she had just left a shrine.

"Will you dress me in your mother's silk qipao?" she said. "I've never dressed like a real woman, not one day in all my life."

"I'll have to get them from Gugu," he said, recalling his mother's wardrobe, filled with silk qipao in every possible color and shade. His aunt had saved it all.

"I knew you in your other life," Sister Wang said, "when you were a pleasant young man who saw the sky as always blue and the sun as always warm."

"You know that man is dead."

"I want to have children with you," Sister Wang cried, "but you are late—you're twenty years too late!" She pulled his hands to her breasts. The two huddled on the table, shivering as if stranded in a barren field. She groped at him like a succubus.

"Do you not still yearn?" she said.

"No one can yearn for the unattainable."

"I'll marry you in my next life," she said, and gripped him harder yet. Her lupine eyes pleaded with him. She wanted him, he knew, even as he knew there was nothing beside him to give himself to.

He had been weeping, he realized, as he pushed himself off the table. His groin ached. He felt Sister Wang had been clutching him for years.

He went to the workstation, a rough cubicle at the end of the hall. A makeshift desk and two bamboo folding chairs took much of the space, though there was room enough, also, for a cabinet and a small iron stove. Three men shared this cubicle—Qing Yuan during the night shift, Qi Chu the morning, and Lao Jia the afternoon. They worked in relays, around the clock, every day of the year.

Lao Jia had started in the morgue when the new government appropriated the hospital in 1949. As for Qi Chu, he'd been a city drifter until he was released from a homeless shelter in 1950 and forced to work as a morgue keeper. He married a peasant woman a few years later. Qing Yuan had been conscripted to the morgue, too, just before Qi Chu, in 1950, after his father had been executed and his mother had died of grief.

Qing Yuan sat at the desk, his eyes shifting from the clock on the wall to the watch his father had gifted him when he graduated from high school.

"The first piece of jewelry a man should own is a good watch," his father had said.

Qing Yuan held the watch to his ear and listened both to the tick of it and the clock and felt himself passing simultaneously through different dimensions, worlds of memories and of ghosts, yesterday's and today's, the life he'd had and the so-called life he now had. The rotten stench of this place, he thought, the countless corpses he had tended, the hours and days and months that had mounted across the sixteen years he'd been here every night—he had made nothing of his time, he thought, he had salvaged nothing, either, absolutely nothing.

Father! he thought. *This watch has conned me of my time. It's never been about carrying on but of giving in.*

There was no life left that wasn't loveless, anymore, Qing Yuan thought. Death was everywhere. Smoke enveloped the city. The ashes from the crematorium chimney covered the streets, sooted the rain, dirtied the snow, damaged the crops, infected every body. It wasn't even ash from coal, he thought, it wasn't even simple dust. It was the remnants of the flesh and bones from every corpse he had cleaned across the years.

Where is your watch, Father? It's your watch I want, yours!

Thirty-seven, he thought again, thirty-seven. He felt almost blessed to have forgotten how each of the corpses had looked or what their cabinet numbers were, but then he remembered them all, the women and the men, the young and the old. They smelled the same, yet somehow each was unique in its way. It was as if the odor of each body told the manner of its death. Then he remembered the baby, too, and pictured it twisted into some nearby trash bin, waiting to be burned.

It was 6:40, and still Qi Chu had not shown. He held two jobs, one cleaning the train station at night, his other the day shift at the morgue. He had three children but no home in the city. He slept a few hours each afternoon in the home of a friend, while his wife and their children waited for him in the countryside. He saw them every few months for a day or two at most.

"The peasants have nothing," he had once told Qing Yuan. "They toil in the fields year after year, yet still they starve."

Qing Yuan seldom complained about Qi Chu's tardiness, but this morning his patience had grown thin. He had felt his rage mounting across the night. He would have fought anyone this very moment, for no reason at all. He shifted a little and fumbled for a cigarette. Truly, he thought, it's terrible to be yourself.

It was almost seven when Qi Chu scuttled in with a lunch bag sewn from an old towel. He neither glanced at Qing Yuan nor apologized for being late. He tossed the bag onto the desk and went to the morgue for his smock. Their work uniform consisted of nothing more than this, a navy-blue smock of heavy fabric, replaced every two years.

Nevertheless, Qi Chu had used the same smock since his first day at the morgue and worn it down to little more than shreds. Each time the old smocks were replaced, he'd send his new one home for his wife to make clothes for their children. Once, Qing Yuan had donated his old smock to Qi Chu's wife. She had used part of it to make three pairs of tiny shoes.

"How many?" Qi Chu said, yawning.

Qing Yuan paused as he went out. "Thirty-seven."

"Busy night."

Death was rarely mentioned in the morgue. Neither he nor Qi Chu nor Lao Jia called the dead by their names but by the number on the cabinet they'd been stored in—3, 17, 31, 12, 19—every corpse turned into a number. Always it was the same, *How many?*

"Only numbers matter," Lao Jia had once said. "We'll all be numbers before we're ashes."

Qing Yuan made his way to the shower, thinking again of the woman who had died of dystocia, her boy stillborn, dead. He had died without ever having lived, he thought. He would never receive a name, much less a number. Soon, Qing Yuan thought, he'd be incinerated as though he were garbage. Thirty-eight, he thought. Thirty-eight.

2.

Just one service window had opened in the canteen hall. The queue, as a result, was long. Nothing anyone said would change things. The people had accepted what they were given, and they waited. Qing Yuan took his place at the end of the queue and lit his cigarette. He and Lao Jia, a few yards ahead, had nodded at each other, but they did not speak. The two had shared breakfast nearly every morning over the years. Sometimes they talked. Others they argued. Sometimes they ate their meals in silence then parted.

Lao Jia had trained Qing Yuan. He had also taught him to drink. Lao Jia carried a flask at all times but, though he sipped from it day and night, seldom lapsed into drunkenness. Now and then he'd lurch into a rage and curse at seemingly anyone, even the nurses he claimed to love. Qing Yuan knew that behind Lao Jia's insolent crafty eyes lay a complex of reckless contradictions, though this did little to ease Qing Yuan's mind. After all these years, the truth was that, depending on the day, he could declare that the man was unreal as easily as he could that he was exceptional.

More than a half hour passed before Lao Jia reached the window. He set his pail on the counter and looked at the fat chef.

"Ticket," the chef said as he stirred the cabbage stew. His eyelids were heavy. He looked half asleep.

"No more till payday," Lao Jia said.

The chef looked up and mumbled. Lao Jia said, "More." The chef scooped a full ladle of stew into Lao Jia's pail and placed a chunk of steamed bread on top. Lao Jia turned away without a word and winked at Qing Yuan as he walked past.

The young doctor behind Lao Jia stepped to the window. "Why did you serve that man without a meal ticket?"

"One more word," the chef said, glaring, "and I'll spit in your food." He poured half a ladle into the doctor's pail. "Now, fuck off."

The doctor slunk away as the crowd laughed and booed, his face contorted with anger and embarrassment.

By and by Qing Yuan got his own food and took a seat beside Lao Jia. His pail was still half full. He'd laid his chopsticks on the rim and leaned back to ogle the two young nurses a few tables off.

"The chef," Qing Yuan said, and bit into his fried dough, "could be the cousin of that giant from the dormitory. Remember him?"

Lao Jia began to slurp again at his stew. He nodded at the chef. "I gave my bicycle coupon to that fatty," he said.

"I thought you wanted a bicycle more than anything? You waited three years for that damned coupon!"

"I did," Lao Jia said. He popped the last bit of bread into his mouth. "Now I don't."

"Why didn't you say something?"

"What do I need a fucking bicycle for? The dorm and the canteen are two minutes from the morgue." He pushed his pail away and lit a cigarette. "And anyway, I like my booze better."

"And he only paid you back with one meal?"

"Of course not," Lao Jia said. "He gave me five yuan. I spent it on booze." He drew out his flask, sipped from it, and passed it to Qing Yuan.

"It's still too early."

"I'm pure proletarian, little brother. And I'm content." Qing Yuan studied Lao Jia's wrinkled face, his sunken cheeks dusty with stubble. Lao Jia burst out laughing. "Tell me, brother, do I own a cabinet? Do I even own a fucking chair?"

"Do you?"

"I don't even own a pair of nail clippers! Why else would I have to borrow yours?"

Qing Yuan detested Lao Jia's borrowing his clippers. He couldn't stand to have anyone touch his toiletries. He couldn't recall the number of times he'd bought Lao Jia clippers of his own, then been told a week or two later that they had been "misplaced." Yet Qing Yuan's compassion for his friend always got the better of him. Not only could he not refuse Lao Jia, but he had given up lending Lao Jia the clippers. Instead, Qing Yuan bought a pair for Lao Jia, then waited for him to finish trimming his nails so he could take the clippers back.

"They pay me enough for a bit of chow every day because they know I'll work till I die."

Qing Yuan stuffed more fried dough into his mouth. He had nothing to say to this and didn't want the conversation to go on. The two had been friends for sixteen years, and yet neither knew much about the other's past. Lao Jia had been a Kuomintang POW. He'd labored for two years in a camp. He had worked in a brothel. That his dossier said as much didn't prove these things. The dossier itself was the truth. More than this, Qing Yuan knew as well that no one in the hospital made less money than Lao Jia. He wasn't even permitted a room of his own in Worker Village.

"I'll die in this shithole one of these days," Lao Jia had said one day, half-drunk. "The rats will eat my flesh." They still shared a bunk bed in the dormitory, then, Lao Jia in the bottom and Qing Yuan on top. "I'm ready for Vimukta right here and now," he had said. "Liberation from suffering. Vimukta, I am waiting."

"Vimukta!" Qing Yuan shouted. "Reincarnation! Nonsense!" He rolled over to see Lao Jia and could just make out an enormous rat scuttling about the dirt floor with three little ones in tow. The rats, he thought, were free, joyous even. They weren't even hungry.

"Death is Vimukta," Lao Jia said from the dark. "If it happens as fast as greased lightning, we are blessed! It's not just Vimukta," he said, "it's 'happy Vimukta.' No pain, no suffering. That's how it will be. Sleep well, little brother."

Qing Yuan couldn't fathom how a man who'd suffered like Lao Jia could want a new life later. He tossed an empty matchbox at the enormous rat. The little ones scattered. The big one, on the other hand, waddled into a dustpan full of cinders and tucked its face under its tail.

"Fuck the bicycle," Lao Jia said, and thrust his pail away. Without warning he tore open his jacket and began to pound on his chest. "Look here, brother!" he roared. "Flesh, blood, and bone! Every piece of me has been eaten away by those corpses. Who can tell me that I—this man, this whole man—doesn't deserve a fucking bicycle?" He took a long pull from his flask and roared again. "Fuck that bicycle! Fuck it!"

Half of the room stopped talking. Some kept their eyes on their meals, though many had turned to stare at the apparent madman. The nurses that just a few minutes before had been gayly chatting turned to Lao Jia, too.

"What the fuck are you looking at?" he said. "Go find some men! Do what you're supposed to. Go get fucked!"

In one motion the nurses rose from their table and fled.

"Calm down, for crying out loud," Qing Yuan hissed.

They sat in silence. Lao Jia sipped from his flask, calm now as a blade of grass, while Qing Yuan finished his meal. He squinted at Qing Yuan. "You look wrong today," he said.

Qing Yuan laughed, baffled by this man before him.

"Have you had a bad night?" Lao Jia said.

Qing Yuan placed the lid on his pail. "I wouldn't say it was good," he said.

In silence both men drew out their cigarettes and lit them with a single match.

"Have we ever had a good one? In that place? How could

you?" Qing Yuan flapped away the heavy smoke. "What does a turtle say when he jumps into a pond?" Lao Jia said, and snapped his spent matchstick in two.

"He?"

"Yes, every turtle is a man, a cuckolded man, no less."

Qing Yuan waited for Lao Jia's answer, but the man said nothing further. "What does the turtle say?"

"'The water is cold.'"

"I don't understand."

"We are the turtles, brother. We jump into the pond every single day, knowing how cold the water will be, and yet we say nothing."

Qing Yuan fished out a few meal tickets and bills and lay them on the table. "Take these," he said.

Lao Jia snatched them up. "I'll get you back on payday."

"I need to sleep," Qing Yuan said, and rose.

The two gathered their things and made their way to the street. Lao Jia turned toward the dormitory while Qing Yuan walked to the bicycle parking lot.

Lao Jia was nearly out of earshot before he stopped and spun around. "How many?"

"Thirty-seven," Qing Yuan said over his shoulder. He thought of the stillborn child and wondered whether he should have included it in the count. Lao Jia would find out for himself, he thought, and waved.

3.

A COOL BREEZE SWEPT down the tree-lined street, droning even at this hour with buses and trucks, the crowds on their bicycles, a unified mass ringing their bells and chattering as one. Beasts labored before their gigantic carts while their masters snapped and barked. Despite the breeze, the air was rank with the odors of garbage, dust, the fumes of diesel and coal.

Qing Yuan bent over in his always futile effort to touch his toes before mounting his bicycle. Yet again, he couldn't reach past his knees. The times he pushed too hard after a shift, he felt his tendons might snap. Fatigue and ache were his longtime familiars. But at least it was sunny. Once again, he had escaped the morgue, for a time. Once again, for a time, he could tell himself the lie that he was free. He looked over his shoulder and merged into the thousands of riders.

The detritus and withered leaves crackled beneath his wheels. It seemed to him they were the croaked whispers of the souls who'd escaped their cabinets in the morgue. He had never liked to admit it, but in such moments he thought it wasn't too farfetched to say he was haunted or insane, which, he thought again, more or less amounted to the same thing. He passed a row of decrepit shops. Everywhere the brick buildings were black with soot.

He had long since given up on the city. Nothing stirred any connection to his past. In fact, he realized, he was wrong to say *he* had given up on the city. The city had given up on *him*, discarded like a dead baby from the hospital the moment he'd been conscripted to the morgue. He existed now in a liminal zone, between a past to which he could never return and a future that would never come. The eternal present, what many a sage declared the one true refuge, had seized him like a spider in its web. He had become a shadow whose life had been bent to a single purpose, the cleaning of humans, dead, on their way to becoming shadows themselves.

Outside the gate of a kindergarten—the Peking Opera House in another life, now enclosed by high walls laced with barbed wire—a long line of teary-eyed children stood waiting for the teachers to let them in. The shriek of a little boy pierced the air—"I want my mommy!"

A medley of bleary-eyed men and women in blue or gray work uniforms shoved against each other as they rushed along. He rode through them, ringing the bell on his handlebar. Across a small public square, a colossal portrait of Mao Zedong bedecked the facade of a government building. Beneath the portrait, a number of lemon-colored slogan-banners rippled in the breeze. None of this had been there yesterday.

At a stop, he watched a blind couple in the white caps made for textile workers shuffle through the pedestrians, many of whom knocked against the couple as they crossed the street. The man waved a long bamboo stick before him with the regularity of a metronome. The woman, bearing a heavy bag on her shoulder, tottered along, gripping her husband's arm.

"Is the bus here yet?" she said. "Is the bus here yet?"

Qing Yuan turned toward the river. A blasting bugle told him a military barrack lurked nearby. No sooner had the bugle ceased than a strident martial composition began to blare from one of the city's untold loudspeakers. This was music of the city.

Near the house he'd grown up in, a church bell used to toll each day. He tried to recall the last time he'd heard it. Now and then he'd pause in the night in the morgue waiting for it to sound, though it never did. It never would again, he knew.

The river lay green and dead. The narrow path along its bank, his shortcut to Worker Village, rolled quietly out before him. Just a few hundred yards from his home, Fan Fan, a crippled woman who had escaped from the countryside during the Great Famine and now scratched out her subsistence begging, stepped from the shadows along some mud shacks and limped with her battered tin toward Qing Yuan. She had been waiting for him, he knew.

Rumors said that Fan Fan had been caught stealing food from a breakfast stall and mercilessly beaten. She herself never confirmed this, even when confronted by some local busybody. She hadn't stolen anything, she once told Qing Yuan, but taken some left-overs from a table at a restaurant, then fallen asleep in an alcove to shelter from a storm. She was fine when she fell asleep, she said. When she awakened, she was "crippled."

She often begged door-to-door at Worker Village. Whenever she knocked, Qing Yuan gave her food from his pail and a few coins. She had memorized his home and his routine and would wait for him. She never failed to address him as "sir," an anachro-nistic expression of gratitude the authorities frowned on but which Qing Yuan nevertheless found endearing. Her merry chattiness both pleased and baffled him. He wondered whether in the dark of a freezing night she felt as alone as he did.

No one knew her real name. All beggars were called "Fan Fan." She never appeared to care. Essentially, Qing Yuan surmised, she had long past dispensed with her ego.

"They can call me whatever they like!" she had said one evening as Qing Yuan poured noodles into her tin. "Names never made much sense to me anyhow. Having enough to eat—that's what matters!"

The times she disappeared for days or weeks, Qing Yuan thought perhaps she'd taken ill or even died. His dread perplexed him as much as Fan Fan herself. He had become inured to death, and yet here, close to his heart, he felt waylaid, stripped of the armor he'd ensconced himself within across the years. In the winter, he often gave her a pint of baijiu in the hopes it might warm her through the night.

Her short greasy hair clung to her head like some hideous foreign hat. Her face was streaked with filth. Qing Yuan knew foul odors well, but her stench was almost more than he could abide. For all of this, she looked up at him and smiled as though he were the sun itself.

He dismounted and took out his pail. "Where have you been?"

"I found a new place, sir," Fan Fan said quietly, "in a school." Qing Yuan opened the lid of his pail and studied her but said nothing. "You're so kind, sir! So kind, so good!" The poor woman's teeth were black, Qing Yuan realized as she spoke, worse than he could remember.

"Which school?" he said, annoyed, despite his tender feelings, that he wanted to know where a beggar slept at night. It wouldn't matter one way or the other. Fan Fan lived in the wild. She had to do what she had to do. He filled her tin then snapped the lid on his pail and put it away.

"Teacher's College in Victory Avenue. Only the Red Guards are there now. They keep to themselves and let me stay in a classroom of my own."

"I've never heard of such a thing."

"I helped them to paste propaganda posters where they told me to. Not just the *dazibao*, but slogan banners, too. I also helped them clean."

"I don't suppose they pay you?" Qing Yuan said, thinking of the poster of Mao Zedong and the slogan banners he'd just passed.

"Food is always good enough for me, sir." She set her tin on the dirt and drew a small red roll from her pocket. "It's the

Red Guard's armband," she said as she unfolded it. "They have an important meeting today, so they locked me out."

Qing Yuan mounted his bicycle and put a foot on a pedal, but Fan Fan stood in his way, staring at him with her ruined eyes. Qing Yuan handed her a ten-cent bill.

"I got married today," she said. "Twenty-five years ago today! I was fifteen. He was eighteen. Those were our good days."

"But where is he now?"

A mournful gleam appeared in Fan Fan's eyes. She had never mentioned her family before. "He's dead. So are our children, all six of them. We starved. I was the only one who made it through." She picked up her tin but didn't raise her head. "But please, sir, don't imagine I'm lonely."

"I hope you can get yourself a drink," Qing Yuan said.

Fan Fan giggled and waved her new bill. "I'll get some baijiu to drink with my husband. Twenty-five years!"

4.

THE OLD GURNEY'S TIRES creaked along the floor outside the morgue. Then the gurney halted. Then a moment of silence fell. Qing Yuan put down his mop and leaned out the door. The body beneath the sheet on the gurney stank of excrement and blood, plus some other odor he couldn't place. The sheet over the body was mostly red.

The masked cleaner who had delivered the corpse handed a form to Qing Yuan without looking up. "I'll come back for the gurney," he said, and scuttled away.

Qing Yuan stuffed the paper into his pocket and yelled. "You can't just leave this here. Do your job!"

The man halted and hung his head. He waited a long moment before shuffling back to push the gurney into the morgue.

"I swear to Chairman Mao," the cleaner said, "she was still gasping just a minute ago. I tell you, those guys are fucking insane! They made me cover her like this even though she was still breathing. They knew she was, I swear! Outrageous!" he shouted. "Outrageous!"

The stench was an entity all its own. Qing Yuan wanted to don a mask himself, something he hadn't done since his first day in the morgue. He lifted a bit of the sheet only to rear back in horror. Never had he felt such visceral shock.

The woman had been slaughtered, he knew straightaway. A butcher couldn't have done a better job. "Where is her family?" he said.

"Family?" the man yelped.

"Who sent her here?"

After years in the morgue, he prided himself on his ability to remain detached, no matter the circumstance. He had been told from the start that the identities of the dead and the causes of their deaths were not his concern, that such questions should never be asked. He had remained loyal to the practice, until now. He was enraged without the means to control himself.

"A streetsweeper found it on the side of the road and brought it to the emergency room in a cart."

"What road?" Qing Yuan said. "Where?"

"I'll come back for the gurney," the man said, and flew away.

Qing Yuan took the form from his pocket. A single, almost illegible word glared at him from the line stating the cause of death: *Trauma.*

He stood between the gurney and the mortuary cabinets summoning the wherewithal to lift the sheet from the body before him. The foulness emanating from it astonished him. He tried to recall another time in his years as a morgue keeper that he had experienced something similar, but couldn't. There was always a first time for everything, as the saying went, he thought, wishing that more than anything the time for this was never.

He left the morgue briefly and returned with a bowl of water. "Just a little wash," he whispered to the corpse. "Someone will bring you clothes by tomorrow."

He took the sheet between a finger and thumb and began to lift it, only to jerk away, again. The sheet may as well have been a house on fire. He couldn't lift it any more than he could touch it.

He summoned his strength and with both hands flung the sheet away. Before him lay a heap of gore and waste unlike anything he'd seen. He touched the corpse. It was still lukewarm. The hair had been chopped down with a razor or a knife. Smashed past recognition, the mouth cleft from ear to ear, every tooth broken or missing, what had once been a face, perhaps even a beautiful face, was now an abomination. The fingernails and toenails, moreover, had been torn away, all twenty of them. And if something could be said to be more heinous, the body, the entire body, every last inch of this poor body, had been smeared with human stool.

Qing Yuan stood before this atrocity dizzy with revulsion and horror. Had he not been clutching the edge of the gurney, he would have collapsed. The room was warping into bizarre shapes. The cords from which the lights hung whirled above him as though a gust of wind had blasted through the room. He had dropped his rag, he realized. The floor was a mishmash of shifting patterns. His foot had become a hoof.

He lurched from the room, down the corridor, and down the second, shorter hall, and then out the front door, where he stopped to suck in great gulps of air. Once he'd regained himself, he lit a cigarette and drew from it one lungful after the next. In a moment it was gone, and he lit another.

How no one had reported this crime astonished him. He wanted to clean the body, but it was nothing that could be cleaned. The concept made no sense, and this alone sent Qing Yuan reeling further. He told himself he would do what he could and returned with a fresh sheet, his gaze to the floor.

He lifted his arms. The sheet floated down. He let go of the sheet. He bowed his head.

"This is my best," he said to the corpse as he slid it into cabinet 19. He closed the door and walked to the workstation and collapsed in a bamboo chair and lit another cigarette he couldn't bring himself to smoke. He smashed it in the ashtray and returned to the morgue.

"I don't know you," he said, his brow pressed to the door of cabinet 19. "I'm not a religious man. I've never believed in reincarnation or any other such thing. But if by chance you somehow return, I beg you to choose to be a butterfly, or a fish, or a flower, or a tree. Never be a human again!" he said, on the verge of weeping.

His body was soaking wet. He could feel his heart in his chest, the adrenaline in his veins. He stumbled to the toilet and stuck his head beneath the spigot. For a long while he did no more than grip the trough and let the water pour around his swaying head. He ran a towel over himself, then returned to the desk in the workstation to complete the form the cleaner had given him with the corpse.

Name: 19.

Gender: Female.

He looked at the little calendar on the wall and scribbled the date: June 6, 1966.

He was still nauseated when Qi Chu rushed in at last, late again, as ever.

"How many?" he said.

Qing Yuan stared at his hand on the table, the little hairs on its back, the veins beneath them, the minute scar he'd gotten as a child jerking his hand from a broken window. For the first time he couldn't remember any of the corpses he'd cleaned that night but for the murdered woman, #19.

"That body," he said, gasping. "#19. I couldn't clean it." Qi Chu looked at him as if he had failed. "But I'm sure someone will send her clothes today."

The shower facilities for hospital employees were in a flat brick house attached to the back of the inpatient building. Mornings were reserved for men, afternoons for women. The house consisted of two hazy rooms.

Qing Yuan went into the changing area and sat on one of the benches. He kicked off his shoes then stood to peel away his clothes. He shuffled into the shower room, dense with steam and the stale funk of mildew and soap.

A young ER doctor, tall and strong, whom Qing Yuan had passed in the hospital three or four times, stood beneath a shower at the end of the room. Qing Yuan waved. The doctor swayed a bit as he waved back. He, Qing Yuan thought, could well be the one who had received #19. He might not have been able to save her—who could have saved her?—yet the man hadn't bothered to do more than write a single terrible word on his form, *Trauma*. If #19 had died of anything, "trauma" had to be at the bottom of the list. The woman had been murdered, out and out.

He opened the taps and waited for the water to warm. But then, of course, he thought, this man might not have been the doctor. There were always several in the ER each night. He could as well have had no idea who #19 was.

After a time beneath the hot water, Qing Yuan's legs began to tremble. He seized the pipe before him, in the clutches of a crippling vertigo. The thought that he ought to return to the morgue to clean and dress #19 ate at him with increasing ruthlessness. The words pounded him—*clean and dress her, clean and dress her*. The room darkened. What had been the clear sound of spraying water had mutated into the howl of a coming storm.

He had been told that the souls of the dead would be forever troubled if they left this world naked and filthy. He had abandoned #19 to just this fate. He had slid her body into its cold cabinet naked and filthy. It was unacceptable, he thought.

He watched the muscular doctor through the steam, savaging himself with a loofah sponge. A compulsive obsession had consumed the man, that much was obvious. He had begun with his face, but once he had scrubbed his body to the toes, he started again at his face. After perhaps three or four rounds of this, the doctor turned to the wall and began to masturbate. Within a minute or so, Qing Yuan heard him moan.

Qing Yuan had done the same himself, countless times, releasing his desire and stress beneath the hot water. It had been some time, however, since he had experienced that puny satisfaction. His lust had been reduced, it seemed, to little more than a gloomy lassitude.

The doctor shut the taps and went to the changing room. Qing Yuan did the same. He watched the doctor drying himself, impressed by his muscular buttocks and back.

"That woman last night," Qing Yuan said, holding his towel before him.

The doctor turned to him. He pulled up his pants and began to button them. "Which one is that?" he said, and slipped into a tee shirt.

"The one who was sent to you in a cart," Qing Yuan said. The doctor's face remained expressionless. "The woman who was slaughtered."

"What about her?"

Qing Yuan couldn't discern a wrinkle of compassion in the man's face, only a sort of arrogant nonchalance. "Was she alive when you received her?"

"Did you know her?"

"It troubles me, is all," Qing Yuan said.

The doctor continued to dress. "That," he said, "is the one thing we doctors don't concern ourselves with—curiosity." He sat on the bench and ran his towel over each foot and then between each of his toes. "*We*, the doctors, couldn't save her. Not as she was."

The same rage that had coursed through Qing Yuan at seeing the word "trauma" on #19's form rushed through him again. *We*. In one swoop, this doctor had immunized himself behind the wall of an anonymous collective. He was no longer a man, but one of the numberless components of a vast organization. Qing Yuan wanted to question him further, but already the doctor had gathered his things and headed out the door.

The doctor was right, Qing Yuan thought. Nothing could have saved that woman. No one could have saved her. #19 could never have been saved. That was the point. Whoever had murdered her hadn't wanted merely to hurt her. They, one man—but how could a single man, if a man it was, though Qing Yuan couldn't fathom a woman disfiguring another woman as #19 had been disfigured, yes, how could anyone in their right mind want to reduce another person to the reeking pulp that Qing Yuan had just slid into a freezing cabinet?—that person, Qing Yuan thought, those people, whoever, had very much wanted #19 not just dead but mutilated past recognition. He tried to imagine the hatred with which one had to have been consumed to do such a thing. He couldn't reach those depths. Not many could, he thought, and took some faint consolation in that truth. Yes, the doctor was right. Then again, it wouldn't take a doctor to know this. #19's fate was evident to anyone with eyes to see.

Qing Yuan sat on the wet bench, listening to the slow drip of water from a faulty pipe. The morgue stunk, but so did this place, somehow. Always a stench followed him, he thought. It was as much his fate to exist in a skulking miasma as it was #19's to have been so viciously murdered. He took his clothes from the peg and started to dress.

5.

THE LINE AT THE canteen had been mercifully short. He saw Lao Jia smoking at a table, his pail nudged away, something he did whenever he'd had his fill. Qing Yuan received his food and with a nod to his friend trudged to his bicycle and made his foggy way home.

He sat at his little table, abject, unaware of what he stuffed in his mouth, then threw himself on the bed. He did not sleep long or well. After a few bites of cold food, he rushed out to buy every paper he could find—the *People's Daily*, the *Guangming Daily*, the *People's Liberation Army Daily*, the *Metropolis Daily*, the *Evening News*. He lay his stack beside him on the stairs outside of the post office and scanned every page until he'd exhausted them all.

Not one of them mentioned the murder of a woman in the night. They featured no more than the ubiquitous propaganda that had sullied them for years, it and the countless unctuous praises of Mao Zedong, the nation's all-powerful savior—political genius, military dynamo, coryphaeus of the Party, The Red Sun, unassailable. Page after page, the dribble went on.

In fact, to Qing Yuan's dismay, not one of the papers mentioned any crime at all. Propaganda had always featured in every major venue, but it had never eclipsed the other sections as it now obviously did. Felonies taken straight from the police blotters had once seemed indispensable to readers. People simply couldn't get enough of the stories about murder, manslaughter, rape, theft, assault and battery, even the bits about runaway children and petty domestic violence. Now, in these so-called newspapers, Qing Yuan found nothing of the sort. There was no "news" anymore. It had been replaced with nitwittery and saccharine blandishment. Fuming, he smashed his cigarette into the photograph of a dour general and tossed his stack over the rail beside the stairs.

Three boys in shorts ambled toward him. Each was barefoot and bare-chested. Each dragged a heavy gunny sack. They stopped a few meters from Qing Yuan and began to study the scene, like crooks the layout of their next heist. Shortly, two of the boys slipped into the post office. The third, quite small, approached Qing Yuan and bowed.

"Sir," he said, "I saw you throw your papers into those bushes. May I take them?"

"There's nothing in them for me."

The boy fished out the papers and stuffed them in his sack. He lingered for a moment, then snatched up the two butts Qing Yuan had left on the stairs. He hadn't gone far before Qing Yuan called him back. The boy returned, his face reddened. "Is anyone you know looking for a woman?" Qing Yuan said. "Or maybe a girl?"

"I don't understand."

"Someone missing."

"They found a girl's body in the river yesterday. Down there," the boy said, and pointed.

"That's not what I'm talking about."

"Your daughter? Or maybe your wife?"

"You seem the sort of young man who gets around," Qing Yuan said with exaggerated cheer. "I thought you might have seen or heard something." The boy stared up at Qing Yuan, beaming. "You'd tell me if you knew, right?"

"I wish I could, sir, honestly I do, but I don't know what you mean."

Qing Yuan waved the boy off. "Of course, of course," he muttered. "Why should you?"

The temperature had peaked, the traffic, as well. Every building was solemn, the shops and stalls grimy with soot to the last. The trees themselves hung black with the stuff. Urchins in rags scuttled here and there. Not a face in the plodding crowds expressed more than grim reconciliation.

Some school children, six or seven years old, maybe, crossed the street, gayly laughing. They were the lucky ones, he thought. He envied their innocence, so otherworldly, so fresh. Then a horse-drawn sewage cart rolled by—these men who transported outhouse waste to the city's hinterland dumps, their carts referred to as *honey wagons*—and Qing Yuan fell numb, as if he had been anesthetized. When he came to, it was with the terrible realization that the stench of the cart was precisely the stench that had oozed from #19.

From the moment he'd awoken, the thought that no one would send #19 her clothes had harried him. He couldn't wait to find out whether she had at least a brother or sister or perhaps even a cousin who'd learned of her death and brought her the best she'd had.

Lao Jia, hunchbacked, was sweeping up the corridor and singing an old folk song. Qing Yuan shook his head with both annoyance and affection. His old friend loved to sing despite his perfect tone-deafness and inability to keep the most basic time. Lao Jia didn't care what others thought. His fellows complained, yet he went on burbling as though he were a canary in a fruit tree. When cleaning corpses, he never failed to hum "The Internationale," almost, it seemed to Qing Yuan, as though the tune were indispensable to the success of the dead in their afterlife. Over time Qing Yuan had come not only to accept his friend's quirk but to admire it. It was one of the few things Lao Jia had left, other than his baijiu, that he could say brought him something close to joy.

"How many?" Qing Yuan said, and Lao Jia stopped.

"Thirteen," he said. He turned to Qing Yuan with a grimace. "This damn corridor is just too long, little brother."

"I'll finish up," Qing Yuan said and made his way to the workstation.

The little room was still dense with Lao Jia's cigarette smoke, and on the desk his pail sat open next to his flask. He'd left some scattered papers and a brimful ashtray. Qing Yuan put his bag in the cabinet, went to the morgue for his smock, then returned to the workstation, where Lao Jia was now resting on a chair, eyes closed, his hands behind his head. Qing Yuan emptied the ashtray.

"That woman," Lao Jia said, "#19. No one sent her clothes."

"Did you try to clean her?"

"I haven't even seen her, and I'm not going to."

"I had hoped someone would at least send her clothes."

"No one is looking for her," Lao Jia said, and opened his eyes. "No one even knows she's dead."

Qing Yuan took a rag from a peg and wiped the pall of ashes from the desk.

"If I were you," Lao Jia said, "I would report this to someone at the Security Department. If you don't, she'll be in that cabinet for a hundred years."

"This is unheard of."

"I've known many people who died alone," Lao Jia said, and nipped from his flask. "I have buried many people. I've fought in wars. I've buried countless dead soldiers. I worked in a brothel and buried—"

"She's not one of those 'many people,'" Qing Yuan said. "She was *slaughtered*."

Lao Jia looked hard at Qing Yuan. "She's as dead as the rest of them." He gestured toward the morgue. "'A morgue is the entry to the cosmos,' it's said. That woman is dancing in the cosmos as we speak. Clothes or no clothes, she is free." Qing Yuan remained silent. Nothing he said would change Lao Jia's view. "Sansan," he said dreamily, "Yuechun, Hongyu, Yiqing, Peilan, Xiulin,

Caifeng, Wenlan." Qing Yuan had heard the names before. They were the women from Lao Jia's long-ago brothel. "Every one of them was a fine whore. But guess what? Each of them died alone."

"What about you?" he said.

"I was there to bury them. I buried them all." Again he looked at Qing Yuan, his eyes now softened. "Whores have everything that makes a woman a woman. There's a reason why their profession is the oldest known to man."

"I've never been. Not once."

"It's a real pity we didn't meet before 1949." Qing Yuan hung the rag on its peg and lit his own cigarette. "There's an exceptional grace in a woman—in all women—that we men will never understand."

"Right now I only want to know why someone hasn't come here with her clothes."

Lao Jia put his flask to his mouth and tossed back his head. Then he turned the flask upside down. It was empty.

6.

At the Security Department Qing Yuan was told by a weasel-faced man that "a report would be filed" for #19. He asked the man precisely what that meant. The man blew smoke in his face and looked at him with his teeny eyes.

"Who will you send it to?" Qing Yuan said. "Can I come back to see what sort of progress has been made?"

"A report will be filed," the man repeated, then stood and walked from the room.

For days Qing Yuan cycled through the city. He scoured train stations, bus stops, street squares, parks, even under the bridges along the river where the homeless gathered at night. He visited every other hospital, every other morgue. He pedaled through both the countryside and the slums, places he'd heard of but never seen. With whomever he spoke, he asked whether they knew anyone looking for a missing woman. He felt hope each morning after his shift, but because no one he encountered knew anything about a missing woman, he went home heavy with disappointment and often, too, despair.

It struck him one day that he had become superstitious. Before going out to the streets, he had taken to saying to himself, *Today will be the day*. By the time he returned empty-handed, he stood before the mirror and looked at the *smack of doom* on his face. *Today I was doomed, but tomorrow it will happen. Tomorrow will be the day.*

He thought of Sister Wang often, wondering if her divination would work for #19. But he'd be damned if he was going to see that charlatan again. He knew that his obstinance, and now his foolish superstition, was at least a part of his suffering.

He'd encountered Fan Fan a number of times since she'd returned but never thought to ask her about #19. As she had done for years, now, one late afternoon she slipped from the shadows along the mud shacks outside Worker Village.

"Fan Fan," he said, after pouring some food into her tin, "would you happen to know anything about a missing woman?"

The poor beggar looked more wretched than ever. "A woman?" she said, startled by Qing Yuan's question.

"Only recently," he said.

"A girl drowned in the river some days ago, is that—"

"Not her," Qing Yuan said, knowing she was referring to the same girl the rag-picker boy had mentioned at the post office.

"There's another?" She scratched her neck, then studied her fingers as if she had snared a louse. "Sir, in such a big city, how would you find her?"

"I know you get about. I just thought you may have heard something here or there."

"People go missing every day, sir," she said, and bared her rotten teeth. "Men, women, children, old and young." Qing Yuan offered her a cigarette. Fan Fan set her tin between her feet and let Qing Yuan give her a light. Two delicate streams of smoke drifted from her nostrils. "She's someone you know? A relative maybe?"

"I can't say."

"Who'd be looking for her if she wasn't missing?" Fan Fan said. Her eyes were alert, now, fiery and blinking.

"She's dead. Nobody has claimed her body."

"Oh, my!" A brief silence passed between them while they smoked. "If she isn't a local, sir," she said matter-of-factly, "it's doubtful she'll have family here."

For all his musing Qing Yuan hadn't considered this. Doubtless she was right. "They found her on June 6th. Weren't you living in that abandoned school at the time, over on Victory Avenue?"

"I'm a tramp, sir," Fan Fan said. "And Victory Avenue is two miles long."

What could Qing Yuan say to that? Fan Fan retrieved her tin, and Qing Yuan mounted his bicycle. "Let me know if you hear anything?"

"Of course, sir," she said, "of course!"

That night, after cleaning, he tapped on #19's door.

"Don't you have any family?" he said. "What about a friend? Are you married? How is it possible you have no one? Why hasn't anyone brought you your clothes?"

He went on talking, pressing his ear to the door as if #19 might reply. He imagined her as a baby, crying in her mother's arms. He imagined her smiling on her father's shoulder. He imagined her as a gleeful girl buying candy at the corner store. He imagined her as a teenager, laughing in a park with friends, as a young woman, sensuous but shy, who blushed when spoken to by a man. She might have been a plain girl, on the other hand. Mutilated as it was, her face had revealed nothing. It was more flesh on a knob on a neck than a face. He couldn't explain his obsession. He'd never wanted to know anything more than he wanted to know the nature of #19's fate, that was all. What was her name? he'd asked himself over and again. None of the names on the list he'd invented seemed right. He could not fathom how anyone could murder a woman like her, with such ruthless depravity.

A week later, a policeman and a woman from the Public Security Bureau arrived at the morgue. Qing Yuan had been enduring double shifts while Qi Chu took time off to be with his wife, who'd given birth to another child, their fourth.

The officer was sickly and thin. His tremendous head and short frail neck gave him the appearance of a hatchling. He strode to cabinet 19 and demanded that Qing Yuan show him the corpse.

He lit a cigarette and began to cough. The moment Qing Yuan opened the door, a stench poured from the cabinet and took the room like an evil fog. The woman, no older than twenty-two or -three, with a flat chest and sharp expressionless face, seemed to have been prepared for this. She brought a handkerchief to her face and squinted. Qing Yuan drew out the corpse. The officer peeled away the sheet, his giant face contorted, then signaled to Qing Yuan to put the body away. The woman slipped the handkerchief under her arm and scribbled in her notebook. Then she hurried out to wait in the corridor. The officer and Qing Yuan followed.

"Where's the paperwork?" the woman said.

Qing Yuan went to the archives room and returned with the form from the doctor and the registration card he had filled out the night #19 had arrived.

"'#19'? Doesn't she have a name?" she said, and handed the forms to Qing Yuan.

"Not that I know of," Qing Yuan said. His exhaustion was his master, now. His mouth wouldn't obey his mind. His tongue had turned into a corpse itself.

"Forget the name," the officer said. "Write what's on the form."

Qing Yuan watched the woman scribble "Name: #19" in her notebook. Two drops of ink leaked from her pen. When she wrote again, the page was smeared along with the side of her hand. This wasn't the first time her pen had failed, Qing Yuan realized. Her hand showed the marks of repeated stains.

"Shall we send her for an autopsy?" she said.

"Why?" The man coughed, then spit a clot of grey phlegm on the floor. The woman closed her notebook. "Put a seal tag on it."

The woman handed a red tag to Qing Yuan and started away. The officer followed, spitting as he went.

Qing Yuan returned to the morgue, drew out #19, tied the tag to its purple toe, and slid the body into the cabinet. "Lao Jia is certain that this place is the entry to the cosmos, and that the stars are brilliant. Have you seen them yet?"

At dawn, #19 was requisitioned as an unclaimed corpse and sent for cremation. Qing Yuan helped the porter, gagging, load the body onto the bed of a dirty tricycle from the Public Security Bureau. He stood and watched the tricycle lurch down the path until it disappeared.

Qing Yuan felt another man inside of him, a weary misanthropist, ashamed, too disgusted to go on living with his fellows. He couldn't bring himself to tell anyone what he'd seen, yet he knew he could neither forget nor ignore it. He was weak, but he was not wicked. He stood on the path in the cool of the dawn listening to the rustling leaves, which, for reasons he couldn't articulate, roused in him not a sense of lightness or joy but only desolation and grief.

7.

"The morgue is closed!" the manager announced. "No one will die today!"

Qing Yuan rushed into the night. He bounced down the snowy streets, filled with inexplicable joy. Every shop, every restaurant was closed. He paused at a corner and gazed at the stars.

Down the way, some windows lit up and music began. The windows were singing, the glass was dancing. His mother's parrots began to mimic her voice, "Happy New Year!" they croaked, "Happy New Year!" And Qing Yuan wept with elation.

His arms and legs were not his own. They had begun to sway with the enchanting music. He couldn't have stopped or controlled himself any more than he wanted to. Humming to the music, he whirled down the street, dense with shadows from the trees. He found himself in the moonlight again.

Fireworks popped in the distance. Then, from the brilliant sky, he heard the sound of marching. He cast about but saw no one. He spun in every direction, circle after circle. He paused at last, dizzy, focusing on the ground to regain himself. When he looked back up, a crowd stood before him, every face familiar as his own.

#3, #27, #36, #15, #16, #29, #32! The dead had escaped the morgue. "Walk with us," they shouted. "You'll never be lonely again! Sway! Dance! March! Come!"

Qing Yuan lurched up sweating. Someone was knocking on his door. He didn't know where he was. He couldn't get out of bed. Then he knew it wasn't his door someone had knocked on but his neighbor's. Two teenagers were arguing in the yard. He glanced at his window and through the thin curtain saw that it was daytime. He shivered as if he were still in the snow, watching the dead dance by. He closed his eyes again and wondered whether his vision had been a hallucination or a dream.

Pots and pans clanked, and plates and spoons clattered from a nearby room. The clock on the nightstand told him it was 12:20 p.m. He had bought the clock years ago but never used its alarm. He sat up and stepped into his shoes. He opened the curtain, the room brightened. He peered about the yard. A few neighbors were coming and going. From a distant radio the Noon-News broadcast a well-known voice he'd been subjected to for years. A woman spoke complainingly. Her husband snapped back then laughed.

Qing Yuan sat on the edge of the bed, winding the clock, which had always run ten minutes behind. *Who's the one getting old?* he thought, and set down the clock. He lit the burner of his small kerosene stove and placed the kettle on it.

"Are you home, brother?" called a woman from his door. He turned and saw, through the glass, Sister Zhou peeking in. The last thing he wanted was to talk to anyone. And yet she had seen him.

She lived next door with her husband and their three children. Her husband was a factory worker. She worked at a breakfast eatery. Qing Yuan had little contact with either of them, beyond the greetings they now and then exchanged.

"Hello!" she said. A short woman in her early thirties, Sister Zhou had a round face and pretty round eyes, and a pleasant voice, as well. "I heard a little noise in your room," she said with a smile, "so I thought I'd stop by."

"Please," he said, "come in." She wanted something, he knew. She had never knocked on his door. This was the first time the two had been alone. He realized when he opened the door and smelled the "clean" air that his room stunk of kerosene. He left the door open, both to freshen the space and to avoid any scandalous gossip that might arise should his ever-alert neighbors see him close the door after Sister Zhou had entered. "Sit down," he said. "Would you like a cigarette?"

She nodded and leaned in for him to light it.

"You shouldn't use a kerosene stove," she said. "So much trouble and expense! You can knock on my door any time you need hot water. Our stove is on all day long."

"I'm used to it," he said. The kettle began to whistle. "I was just making tea. May I offer you a cup?"

"Please don't trouble over me!"

"It's as easy to make two cups as to make one," he said, and spooned the tea into his little pot. He could see her scanning the sparse room. He had a single bed, a nightstand, a table, two chairs, a small desk near the corner. The floor was dusty. The ashtray was full. It had been weeks since he had cleaned. Scouring the city for news of #19 after his nightly shifts left him with no energy but to eat and sleep. Sister Zhou's inquisitive eyes disturbed him. He felt outright awkward, alone with this woman in his dour room.

"I apologize for the mess," he said, and set two cups on the table. "I meant to clean yesterday, but I've been too busy and tired."

"Brother. You work year-round without a break. I can't imagine you'd have enough energy to clean more than twice a year!"

"Not to mention how hard it is to sleep in the day."

"You're telling me! I got up at 2:30 this morning and haven't rested for a minute since. I suppose I really could do with a cup of tea."

He sat down and waited for her to say why she'd come. A woman in the yard stopped before the door and peered in. A single man and a married young woman, alone in a room, talking and having tea—that would make for some juicy gossip, all right.

Sister Zhou leaned in to blow on her tea. She picked it up and began to take quick small sips. "Brother, you know me well enough. I'm not the nosy type. But when something so tragic has happened, I have to share it." She looked at him as if for permission to go on. "You know the Tongs, right?

"Barely."

"Feng Ge's husband died. Well, actually he was killed."

Qing Yuan raised his brow as if to say, "Oh, dear!"

"I'm surprised you didn't know."

"I had heard something like that," he said, "only I didn't know the specifics." About a week ago, in the latrine, he had overheard two men speaking in hushed voices. A neighbor, one told the other, had been killed in the street. Qing Yuan couldn't say whether this was the truth or, as too often, hearsay. No more than the words "neighbor" and "killed" had stuck with him.

"Well, it's true," Sister Zhou said. "It was Feng Ge's husband. He was killed," she repeated. The way she spoke about Feng Ge insinuated that Qing Yuan had known her for years. He may have passed her once or twice in Worker Village but had little recollection who she was. He could, on the other hand, recall her husband—a tall swarthy young man impressively muscled. In summer, he had stridden about bare-chested, showing off his powerful figure. He reminded Qing Yuan of a kung fu master from some martial arts novel. "Such a shame that a tough fellow like him could pass away in the blink of an eye," Sister Zhou said, and sighed. "I can't help but to think that sometimes a man can be as frail as a mosquito! One swat might not kill a mosquito, but it can surely kill a man."

"Was he by chance a martial arts master?" Qing Yuan said, like a boy.

Sister Zhou looked both surprised and pleased at Qing Yuan's interest. "Feng Ge told me that as a child he'd trained with his grandfather." She sipped her tea and rushed on. "It's such a coincidence that you wouldn't believe it. Feng Ge and I work together, and for a time her husband and mine were colleagues in the same machinery plant. We were born in the same year, too. In fact, so were our children. The only difference is that she has two daughters and a baby boy, and I have two sons and a baby girl. Strange, right?" She laughed, a quirky laugh, Qing Yuan thought, and continued to scrutinize him. He forced himself to smile. Yet he couldn't bear her gaze for long and looked down at his tea.

"But it's so horrible to know he died in such an awful way. It's hard to imagine how devastated Feng Ge is," Sister Zhou said, and pursed her lips.

The image of #19 on the bed of the porter's tricycle came to mind. He could even smell the terrible stench of her. Death was everywhere in his life, he thought. He was a steward of death, in fact. He refilled Sister Zhou's cup.

"I'll share this with no one but you, brother," she said, and leaned closer to Qing Yuan. "I've never mentioned it to Feng Ge," she whispered. "I don't want to hurt her feelings. As I said, my husband knew her husband well. He was a nice guy, my husband says, but a little ardent, a little overheated by the politics, perhaps even a bit too ambitious. I hope you appreciate that it may not be quite proper to talk about him in this way. I'm sure you know what I mean." She smiled again, as sweetly as if she and Qing Yuan were brother and sister. She sipped her tea, then went on. "But he triumphed. He infiltrated the radical faction and became a Party member. He was quickly, perhaps too quickly, promoted to be a propaganda cadre in the Municipal Machinery Bureau. An enormous step up! A rising political star, no doubt about it.

"So! An exciting time for him," she said, "and a big change too—from factory worker to Party office man. They even paid for his lunch and dinner. But of course it didn't last long. He and his comrades were hanging slogan banners on the bureau building one day, and a fight started with some men in the conservative faction."

"Over banners?" Qing Yuan said, wondering how much of this was true. Who would fight over a couple of stupid banners? The notion was ridiculous.

"It's true, brother," she said. "All true. The fight went on till suddenly, as if from nowhere, a fellow sprang up behind him and smashed his head with a spade." She paused, almost hyperventilating. She had been talking in a harsh rapid whisper, acting the scene out as if she were telling a ghost story to children.

Her hair shone darkly in the mellow light. Until today, he hadn't noticed how pretty she was. It was her eyes, he thought, so compellingly round. But all this killing—he was sick of it. He imagined the young man slumped in the dirt like a shot beast, blood spilling from his head. He couldn't help but to think of #19 again, slaughtered, and in all likelihood for much less than Feng Ge's husband had been killed.

"So he died," he said.

"Yes," she said, and leaned in close enough that Qing Yuan thought she might lay a hand on his knee. Tiny beads of sweat had appeared on her nose. "Yes, yes, right then and there. He was probably dead by the time he hit the ground. They didn't even send him to a hospital—straight to the morgue!" Sister Zhou sighed, as if exhausted. She looked into Qing Yuan's eyes. "Harrowing," she said, now in tears, "absolutely harrowing."

"Truly terrible," Qing Yuan said. The afternoon sunlight had cast a bright line across the floor. Motes of dust swirled through it. He looked to the window and saw it was cracked.

"Feng Ge's children have probably suffered more than she herself. She's done what she can, gone to any number of government sections, begging for mercy at them all. No one could say her family wasn't owed *some* compensation." She dropped her voice still more. "Brother, you'd have thought such a request was perfectly reasonable, but not those heartless officials! A temporary job at our eatery was all they gave her. Shameful!"

The neighbor who had peered in at them was still lurking. She stepped into the doorway and stopped. "Sister Zhou," she said, "it must be nice to have so much free time for cigarettes and tea!" Then, instead of leaving, the woman slouched against the frame and stared. "What's the big secret?" she said. "What have you two been whispering about?"

Qing Yuan had seen the woman twice at most. They had never spoken. "Please come in and join us," he said as he approached her. "A little tea? A cigarette?"

"As you can see," the woman said, "I have no time for chatting." She did, however, have time to take Qing Yuan's cigarette. "Thanks for your generosity," she said after he lit it, and shuffled away with a sneer.

"What a piece of work," Sister Zhou said.

Qing Yuan made every effort to remain placid. He had nothing to offer but cigarettes and tea. He offered both again, and she thanked him with her pleasant smile. The longer she sat beside him, Qing Yuan thought, the more lovely she became.

"Feng Ge is quiet," Sister Zhou said. "Better yet, and you don't find this virtue in many people these days, women or men, she's *genuine*. What's more, she's dexterous and skilled. She knits and sews everything. And none of this is to mention her beauty! When it comes down to it, brother, she is a perfect woman. Well, she would be if her husband hadn't been killed. How terrible!"

Having spent her time talking about the death of Feng Ge's husband, and then of Feng Ge's struggles and charms, he sensed Sister Zhou working toward a request related to the young widow. Sister Zhou had more than aroused his pity. His heart had been shattered for years. How could he not pity the world itself, despite his conflicted misanthropy, his disgust at a frailty so profoundly embedded in human beings, as if without it we wouldn't be humans at all—oh, the irony! he thought. How could he not lament that despite all its accomplishments humanity was still doomed to fall by its own devices?

His own life had been Miltonian, he thought. He was not just a man whose paradise had been taken. For no clear reason, he had then been cast into the hell of his life as a morgue keeper for these last sixteen years.

Something in everyone, he'd learned tending *his* corpses—*his* corpses! his!—had been forever broken. Most did not know this. They hadn't seen it. But Qing Yuan knew. He saw it every night, seven days a week, month on month, year after year. This was what he knew, and what he knew, he realized, was what he had become.

#19 had broken something deep inside him he hadn't known was there to break. She had been a human once, good or bad, it made no difference. She had been utterly desecrated, utterly destroyed, then sent to him as though she were toxic waste. No one had come to claim her. No one had sent her clothes. She'd been trundled off on a dirty tricycle by a sad man whose life, like Qing Yuan's, amounted to ferrying the dead from this sad world out into a cosmos that, as Lao Jia never failed to insist, was waiting for us all.

The single hope that remained to Qing Yuan lay in this alone. He had always wanted to believe this, that in fact a splendid cosmos glistening with an infinity of stars waited for each and every one of us, into which, good or bad, we'd be released, freed from the chains of our impoverished existences on this unforgiving planet.

For an instant it occurred to him he could lurch up and smash everything in sight. It wouldn't take long, he knew, in this sparse room. He knew as well that such recklessness would do little to ease him. He smiled at Sister Zhou. She'd reach her aim soon enough.

"I'm the one who has persuaded Feng Ge to remarry," Sister Zhou said, and Qing Yuan understood. "She's far too young and attractive to be a widow for the rest of her life. She has three children. Everyone knows the difficulty of the stepfather of a widow's children," she said and stopped to study Qing Yuan again, as if to say, *Now you know why I'm here.* All that remained was for him to hear out her case.

"Kids," she said, "can be hard to win over, especially the older ones. They're manipulative, even treacherous. Why would a man choose to trap himself in such a place? But, brother, it's important to consider the matter from a broader perspective. Feng Ge is much younger than you, and she is beautiful! Were you two married, there's still the chance you could have your own child! And I can assure you Feng Ge will make the very best wife. Imagine coming home from work to find your house clean, your dinner ready, your clothes washed and folded! Imagine the warmth of a bed at night in the cold of winter. How nice would all of this be?"

Sister Zhou had done her homework, that much was plain. To learn his age alone would have necessitated she examine the records at the Community Committee. She might even have visited the police station. And that had to have been but a start. This woman was clever, Qing Yuan knew. She had planned everything to the minutest detail.

"Mama! Mama! Where are you?" Sister Zhou's daughter was calling from the yard. Shortly she appeared in the doorway, as if chased by a lion.

"I'm here, baby," Sister Zhou said, and rushed to the little girl.

"Please," Qing Yuan said, relieved at the interruption, "come in!"

Sister Zhou scooped the child up and returned to her seat.

"Be good now, and say hello," Sister Zhou said. The girl had buried her face in Sister Zhou's arm and wouldn't look up.

The child turned her face a little toward Qing Yuan. "Uncle, hello!" she said.

This warmed Qing Yuan. He went to the cupboard, opened a tin, selected a handful of candy, and gave them to the girl.

"Oh, my goodness," Sister Zhou said. "How generous!" The child had metamorphosed into a cheerful gremlin, picking through the candy to see which she'd gobble first. "Don't eat that until you thank him properly."

The girl thanked him and began to unwrap the piece of candy she'd selected. It both gladdened and embittered Qing Yuan to see her. Without doubt the room had brightened as if a rainbow had appeared in it. Yet the light couldn't dispel the shadow of sorrow that for years—since he'd become a morgue keeper—he'd avoided considering the possibility of having his own child. He wondered if the girl's sudden appearance was the closing phase of Sister Zhou's argument. Either way, it was working. Maybe, at last, the time had come for him to think about starting a family.

"She's a lot taller than when I last saw her," Qing Yuan said.

"Sometimes I think they look different every day. They steal our time, that's for sure."

The girl slipped the candy she'd unwrapped into her mouth then pocketed the rest. "I want to go home now," she said.

"In a minute, okay?" Sister Zhou said.

"I can get there myself," the child said, and wriggled free.

"Fine," Sister Zhou said as the girl danced off. "But don't gulp down all that candy. Save some for your brothers!"

She turned back to Qing Yuan and her tea. "Incidentally," she said in a way that Qing Yuan thought dramatic and conspiratorial, "Feng Ge is quite familiar with your *situation*." He didn't need a translator to understand. *A morgue keeper isn't a normal job, and it is far from enviable.* "But Feng Ge is a good woman," she added, as if to say the woman wasn't simply lovely and kind but charitable, as well. "To her," Sister Zhou said, and drew closer than Qing Yuan would have liked, "nothing matters as long as a suitor is a gentleman and willing to treat her children as his own."

Qing Yuan blushed. The proposition, its sheer abruptness, had thrust him into near senselessness. He couldn't say it was unwelcome. From nothing, another day in a line of days that a long while back had melded into a single day, he'd been tendered this strange and wondrous proposition.

Sister Zhou put her cigarette in the ashtray and set down her cup. Qing Yuan couldn't bring himself to look at her again. He didn't want to make a fool of himself. He didn't want to insult her and by extension Feng Ge. He didn't want to do anything that might jeopardize this potentially marvelous opportunity. The slightest movement could break the spell, he thought. He'd blink and find himself alone in a dusty room. Some child in the yard would cry out. He'd see the motes swirling through the sunbeam through his window. His stove would still be burning. The two sat in silence.

In all these years it hadn't occurred to him he might find a woman who'd care enough to marry him. Before his father had been killed and his mother had died, before his world had been destroyed, it had seemed a matter of course that marriage and a family would manifest in due time. He'd had a fiancé, once. He'd been set to inherit his father's jewelry concern. A happy life had been preordained, he'd always felt. Then came Mao Zedong, and then came disaster and death with its servants, misery and grief.

After a time Sister Zhou stood and pushed her chair to the table. "Thank you so much, brother," she said, "for your generosity. Thank you for hearing me out. Please know the last thing I want is for you to think I've been presumptuous. I'm only trying to make things right for people I care about. I'll let you consider my suggestion, okay? There's no pressure. Just let me know when you're ready."

Still Qing Yuan didn't speak. The finest web seemed to have bound his eyeballs to his toes. He rose staring at his feet and shuffled to the door, Sister Zhou before him. She stepped into the yard. "Thank you, again, brother. I know you are a kind man."

He shut the door and began to clear the table. A tiny stained chip on the brim of Sister Zhou's cup seemed to glare at him with disdain. Sister Zhou had seen it, he knew. Yet she had said nothing. Mortification shot through him. Gratitude tempered it. Sister Zhou's discretion was another reflection of her kindness. He stared at the cup, like a man deep in contemplation. After a time, his chin jutting in disgust, he flung the thing into the trash.

Above the washstand hung a small mirror. Dark circles hugged his eyes. He had allowed a beard to consume his face. Again, the words *smack of doom* leapt to mind. He sniffed about. The odor of the dead had infested him as surely as the beard had taken his face. He had stumbled through this ritual many, many times, but always forgot it until he found himself in its midst again, always realizing the same old thing. He'd never rid himself of this smell, he knew.

He opened the shaving kit his mother had given him some two decades back. Years had passed since he'd been able to find proper razor blades. He'd had to settle for cheap copies from the Soviet Union. He worked his soap into a lather on his neck and face then sliced away the offending hair. Then he toweled himself clean and examined himself, surprised to find a man to whom time hadn't been as pitiless as he had imagined, with eyes he considered more fearless and determined than he had minutes before told himself they were.

8.

Late evening, a moonless night, a chorus of stars shimmered into the distance. Qing Yuan rode down the path along the river. A few youngsters squatted in the glow of a streetlamp on the bluff. One whistled a famous love song. The others listened as they smoked. He passed on, light with what he remembered as joy. The path narrowed and grew bumpy. A young couple beneath a willow tree embraced, deeply kissing.

He stopped at a corner store. Above the single open window, a kerosene lamp swayed in the breeze. Long ago, before the liberation, the place had been a charming gift shop where his mother had shopped for handkerchiefs and gloves. The first birthday gift he had given his mother, when he was five, had been a silk handkerchief. The maid had embroidered his name on it. His mother had wept when she unwrapped it.

Now a sweaty middle-aged woman was cooking on a small stove against a wall streaked with soot. The food smelled terrible, Qing Yuan thought, offal of some sort, no more than waste, he knew. Her wet shirt gripped her breasts like paint. He could see her nipples. He asked for two packs of cigarettes and a bottle of baijiu. A shaggy mole hunkered on the back of her hand, he couldn't help but to see when she handed him his things.

He pedaled off through a loose gang of begging tramps and thought Fan Fan might be among them. She had disappeared again.

When he reached the morgue, its door hung wide open. The stench that emanated from it, he thought, was the same stench he'd been working through for days. Lao Jia stood outside, smoking amidst a cloud of flies he hadn't bothered to notice. A masked cleaner wheeled out a barrow heaped with soiled sheets. He settled the barrow on the path then returned to hand a form to Lao Jia.

Lao Jia took a pen from his pocket, signed the form, then thrust it back to the man. "Do you know why this place stinks like fucking shit?" he said and nodded at the barrow. "Because your lumpy ass hasn't collected that crap for a week."

The man gathered the wheelbarrow and pushed away.

"How many?" Qing Yuan said.

"That fucking asshole," Lao Jia said. "I've been sick all day because of those sheets." As though he'd noticed them only now, he waved at the flies. "What's wrong with you? You look, I don't know, *different*."

"I shaved," Qing Yuan said.

"Nope. Something else."

Qing Yuan passed into the morgue to gather his smock. Then, in the workstation—he couldn't believe it—he found Lao Jia at the desk shoveling cabbage into his mouth. How anyone could think to eat in this rotten air astounded Qing Yuan. He pointed at a new portrait of Mao Zedong on the wall.

"Who put that there?"

"Some guys from the Labor Union came this morning. They told Qi Chu every room has to have one." He put the lid on his pail and scrutinized Qing Yuan. "What's really going on? Other than that you shaved." Qing Yuan shook his head and collected the papers on the desk. "Is this about a woman?" Lao Jia said and guffawed. "Is that what this is? Did you get yourself a woman?" Qing Yuan emptied an ashtray into the bin. "Now you're blushing," Lao Jia said.

"I got this for you," Qing Yuan said, and set down the bottle he'd just picked up. "Do you want a drink?"

"Only if you tell me the truth."

Qing Yuan filled two glasses. Then, inasmuch as he'd intended not to, he found himself telling Lao Jia everything Sister Zhou had said about Feng Ge, absent the part about her murdered husband.

"I'm happy you found yourself a woman."

"It's too early to—"

"Listen to me, little brother. A man *needs* a woman. You may not have children, but you have to have a woman. You need her warmth. You need her curves and her scent. Forget her appearance. When you turn off the light, they're all the same."

How Lao Jia could pester him to get married without having done so himself amused Qing Yuan. Lao Jia had been alone since they met. "Where's your woman, old man?"

Lao Jia's face radiated with innocent perplexity. He couldn't see himself, Qing Yuan knew. The man had no idea how hollow his heart had become. "Women, children—family—that's what we men want and love. Don't get me wrong. I'm not saying you should marry any old woman. She has to be a good one, someone who can feel for you, who can read your mind. She has to be the one you can share your secrets with."

Lao Jia held out his empty glass. Qing Yuan filled it and rose to stretch his legs. "So, like I was saying, where's your own wife? What's keeping you?"

"I was married," Lao Jia said. In a flash he'd turned somber. "That was a long time ago."

"You never told me that."

"Brother, you and I aren't the kind who run around yakking about what we've lived through." Qing Yuan looked into Lao Jia's anguished eyes. "I was once a warrior. I never smoked, I never drank, I hardly even smiled. My wife and I had only been married three years when I went to fight the Japanese. We'd already had two boys." He paused, musing. "I'm not boasting, but I was a killer. They promoted me to company commander. I did my duty like I was told, with never a complaint. Then one day I got a letter from my cousin. The Japanese had burned down my entire village and raped every woman in it, my wife included. They killed my boys. That very night I deserted. Everything, honor, glory, pride, all of it had become meaningless. I hid in woods and caves by day and traveled by night. I stole food. I ate plants, tree bark, anything I could get. I didn't know where I was going. The only thing I cared about was that no one knew me. And then I ended up here."

Qing Yuan sat before his poor friend, appalled, wondering how all these years he could have kept such a terrible secret. His friend had lived with unspeakable sorrow and grief, and he had never guessed it. He didn't know what to say or do more than light another cigarette and drink.

"I wished she'd died," Lao Jiu said.

"What?"

"Don't look at me like that! A young woman, my *wife*, the mother of my *children*, gang raped by soldiers? It was too much to bear." Shame gnawed at Qing Yuan. Who was he to judge a man who had endured the unspeakable? "It took a while," Lao Jia said, "but that's when I got my job as a gatekeeper for the brothel. I wanted nothing more than to forget everything. I still do."

"You never saw your wife again?"

"I don't know how she found me, but she did. She said nothing, not a word. She just stared at me till I could no longer bear it and asked why she had come. She wanted me to go home with her. I refused. She asked if she could stay with me. I refused that, too. I looked away, ashamed, and when I looked back, she was walking out the door. I was weak. My shame haunts me to this day."

Qing Yuan offered Lao Jia another cigarette. Neither man spoke for a while.

"They found her a few days later," Lao Jia said, after he'd

mashed his nubbins in the tray. "She'd drowned herself in the river. No one can explain these things, but somehow I was passing by just then. She wasn't recognizable, the river had eaten her up, but I knew it was her by her clothes." His eyes were filling with tears. "I don't believe in coincidence anymore," he said. "God had wanted me to see what I had done."

He stared at his tattered shoes, his wrinkled face glittering. Then, wincing, he clinked his glass against Qing Yuan's and drank. Qing Yuan knew that any word he spoke would amount to blasphemy. In his head he heard the sound of a river surging his way.

"It's the weakness of man," Lao Jia said, his smile as sad as any Qing Yuan had seen.

"It's the weakness of man that's saved you, my friend."

A thin line of snot hung from Lao Jiu's nostril. He pressed a thumb to the other and blew the snot out, then wiped his hand on his shirt.

"I may wish I were dead, but since I'm not, there's nothing to do but live as best as I can." With his knuckle he began to tap a beat on the desk. "Sustain, little brother," he said, smiling with profound sadness. "Sustain! All we need to forget about everything is a good night of fucking."

9.

He knew it was her the moment he entered the park. She sat on a bench, her back straight and legs crossed, holding a knee with both hands. The park had once been a wealthy family's private rock garden. The rocks were still there, multicolored and jagged, accentuating the wildflowers and trees lining the gravel path. A few other couples lounged about holding hands as they chatted. She saw him and bowed her head. She was shy, he saw. Right away he liked her. Their eyes met, yet neither could do more than stumble through muttered greetings.

"I hope you haven't been waiting long," he said, and sat on the bench beside her, though not too close.

"Not at all," she said.

"Is it true you go to work at three-thirty in the morning?"

"And at three on weekends."

"Is it safe to walk alone that early?"

"Sister Zhou and I always go together."

"But what about your kids?"

"I worry much more about my oldest daughter than about my baby boy. She goes out with kids I don't know and sometimes doesn't come home till after dark. She's the captain of a platoon of Little Red Guards and the co-leader of its propaganda team. She's like her father, far too zealous for an eleven-year-old."

"I saw your other daughter at the tap last week," he said.

"How did you know it was her?"

"My sixth sense," he said, and winked. It was true, of course. He had gone to fetch water and noticed a girl of six or seven washing clothes in the wooden basin. She'd rolled her sleeves up to her elbows, a child fiercely scrubbing clothes without pause. As he drew nearer, he could see her hands, both of them riddled with scabs.

"It must have been her. I don't know what we would do without her. She does everything, cook, wash, clean. I've never asked her to do any of it. She just does. And she gets up every morning to see me off."

The child's hands had disturbed Qing Yuan since he'd seen them. He ached at the thought that the poor girl must be suffering. Feng Ge might be sensitive to the matter, but he felt it better to let her know his feelings sooner than later. "This is a bit awkward for me," he said, "but may I ask what's troubling her hands?"

"Chilblains," she said, grateful, it seemed to him, that he had noticed.

"Has she seen a doctor?"

"The doctor at the Children's Hospital prescribed a cream. It helped a little, but then it came back."

"There's a dermatology department in our hospital," he said. "They have specialists. Maybe you could bring her?"

"I didn't know that. Thank you."

"Do you mind if I smoke?" he said. She smiled and shook her head. Her beauty continued to strike him. "Would you like one?" She hesitated before accepting. He struck a match and held it out. She leaned in closely. The skin of her neck was flawless. He swooned at the scent of her hair.

"I only ever smoke with Sister Zhou," she said. "During our breaks."

Through the trees they could see the sun meeting the horizon. Clouds had piled up along a rim of shifting pink and gold, the sky above a deepening blue.

They'd been silent, mesmerized. "How beautiful!" she whispered.

"So," he said.

"I haven't been in a park for years," she said.

"1949," he said. "That was the last time for me. On Lotus Birthday."

"I never knew that the lotus had a birthday," she said.

"June 24th," he said. "When I was a student, my university used to hold a dragon regatta on Lotus Birthday every year," he said. "I raced with the team. The year we won, we celebrated in a restaurant on the river and got into a fight with the guys who lost. We were all too drunk and got our asses beaten. A guy kicked me into the river. I went home like a half-drowned dog."

She laughed, and he laughed with her. They leaned back, more relaxed now.

Something unexpected was happening, he knew. How different everything felt tonight! For years, his life in the morgue had been his one reality. He had been mashed into a wretched creature. He had ignored what he saw. He'd hidden behind the curtains of his dingy room in Worker Village. When seized by despair, he had skulked to the morgue and like a madman babbled to the dead.

But here, now, next to a woman who laughed with authentic delight and talked with true serenity, everything had changed. Yes, he had lost so much. Yet it didn't have to stay this way. Here he sat talking and acting not like a wretched morgue keeper but like the man he once had been. He could feel it. He knew it was true by the sound of his voice, dynamic and melodic, by the effect of his smile on the woman beside him. Already he had endeared himself to her. His rapture at the possibility of a new life with her and her children was soaring. He could find peace with his past, he could see a different future, happiness and contentment, even zeal.

She, too, had become herself, affectionate, admiring, alluring, gay. She had gazed into his eyes when he lit her cigarette. She had let him see her attraction. And it was genuine for a reason—he was elegant, his tenderness was real. Her own charms were also true, her smooth sleek face, the tilt of her nose, her voice, so supple, her intoxicating aroma, her shyness. His banter had enchanted her. She laughed at his jokes. She teased him, too, and murmured with him as he spoke—*That's funny!* and *How silly you are!* and *Oh, my goodness, really?* Her hand brushed his knee. She asked his forgiveness, but he knew she had touched him on purpose.

"I have to say," she said, "I couldn't remember what you looked like before you came."

"I wouldn't have expected you to," he said. "I remember you, but only faintly. We haven't seen much of each other, you know." They were both a bit embarrassed, both more than a little shy. "I met your husband once and smoked with him," he said.

Her face in the falling dusk was wonderful and pale. "What did you talk about?"

"Nothing serious," he said. "We shared a moment smoking."

"He liked to talk and could get along with anyone, even the tramps. There was one he talked to all the time, the beggarwoman who makes her rounds in Worker Village. Do you know the one?"

"Fan Fan?"

"That's her. He knew everyone in Worker Village."

"May I ask how you found out?"

"I don't understand."

"What happened to him?"

Her face palled, and straightaway he knew he'd gone too far. What a foolish question to ask this first time with her, courting her, it struck him, trying to win her over. She looked away and with two trembling fingers caressed her temple. He watched her, lashing himself for having committed this blunder.

After a moment she set both feet on the ground and straightened her back. Her head rose, too. Her face—he couldn't think of a better word—had steeled. She had decided something, though he couldn't say what until she began to speak.

"He didn't come home that night," she said, and he understood that she had refused to let her tragedy define her. "That wasn't unusual. He often worked so late he'd sleep in his office. I didn't find out till the next evening. One of his colleagues came to our house. He explained that after a meeting the night before, my husband had gone home alone. But when he didn't show up in the morning, his colleagues began to worry. Shortly after that, the police called to say his body had been found on the street."

His heart ached for this woman. She had endured too much. Everyone, he thought, had endured too much—Lao Jia, Qi Chu, Feng Ge, himself, surely himself and his family, and every last body sent to him at the morgue, all of whom had once been people, people who had suffered and suffered terribly, and the people suffering whom the dead had left behind, and, of course—more than the rest, he believed, though who really could say—#19.

He turned full to her. He wanted to take her hand but didn't. "We don't have to talk about this anymore if you don't want to," he said, striving to fill his words with his whole heart. "I'm sorry to have been so insensitive."

She had the face of a Guanyin, he thought, gazing at her, that mélange of beauty and profound sorrow. Her grief had become her power, he realized. Her tragedy had made her stronger. Her melancholy was noble. She turned to him and looked into his eyes.

"But I want to," she said. "I haven't spoken about it once. I didn't know till now, but it's something I needed to do."

A burden was lifted. He had been absolved. His gratitude was immense. He felt for a moment that his tenderness for this woman could destroy him. She was beautiful, he saw with total clarity, her heart, her body, her mind. One word alone captured her essence—*exquisite.*

"Apparently," she said, going on with her tale, "it was some Red Guards who found him. They brought his body to a morgue then reported it to the police. His belongings were still with him, they said, his bag, his wallet and employee card. They said that ruled out his having been killed by some deranged mugger. And anyway, it's doubtful that would ever have happened, that he'd have been killed by a single man. He knew very well how to defend himself."

Qing Yuan felt himself split inside, without knowing why. Then he recalled Sister Zhou's version of this awful thing. It had been quite different than what he was hearing now.

"Then what was the cause?"

"They said he'd been in a fight. I asked about his wounds, but they insisted he had none. He *just died*," she said. "That's what they said. He *just died*. I couldn't understand. I was numb with disbelief and rage. I hadn't thought for myself. I could only think about my children, and how we were going to survive." She gazed into the growing dusk.

"I'm so sorry," he said.

A couple passed, hand-in-hand. He said hello. They smiled and went on, murmuring.

He leaned back to watch her and thought again about how much she had endured, and of her fortitude to carry on. Some unseen strength had buoyed her up. His admiration was profound.

Almost to herself, she said, "I still doubt what they told me."

"What about the Red Guards who found him?"

"The police claimed not even to know their names."

"That's absurd," he said. "Do you think they were trying to hide something?"

She fretted at her blouse, observing it with reasonless intensity. "'They just happened to be there.' That's what the police said."

"It's absurd," he said again, apoplectic. "It's absurd, just absurd." It took him a moment to gather himself. "Were you able to see him? You know, before—" He didn't know the proper words— "took him away," "sent him off," "cremated him," "burned him." Yet she understood.

"In the morgue of the funeral home," she said. "We were ordered to stand in line, two meters away. I couldn't really see him. He wore a cap, and they had covered him to the chin with a sheet. He looked peaceful enough, I guess." She was crying now. His heart ached for this woman in her agony. "His colleagues had also come," she said. "The morgue was small, so it was full. There were no windows. It was cold and dank and the light was dreadful. And the stench. I've never smelled anything like it."

Several fingers on one of his hands began to twitch. He slipped the hand under his thigh. "A morgue is supposed to be windowless."

"Who said that?"

"It's what I've been told. Lao Jia says it's because the souls of the dead would escape. They'd wander forever in agony and grief, beyond any help, he says. He talks about it all the time. The morgue, he's always saying, is the gateway to the cosmos. He says a lot of things like that."

"I took my three kids, also," she said. "They were much stronger than I had thought they'd be. Not one of them cried. I don't think it was because they felt nothing. It's because they felt too much. They loved him. He was their comfort and their protector. I knew if I didn't bring them they'd despise me once they were old enough to know." She bowed her head. Her cheek was wet. "It's them who keep me going," she said.

He slipped a handkerchief into her hand. He was powerless. Even so, all he'd felt from the moment they met had stayed with him, the light, the hope. She hadn't held back. She'd trusted him, she'd made herself vulnerable. He couldn't speak for her, but she may have been as grateful as he was. He knew *he* was grateful. They had much more in common than petty need. They shared indescribable pain. They had loved, they'd been loved, they had triumphed, they had lost. They were still alive. They wanted still to live, and more, to love again, despite.

10.

It had been a windy spring, without a day of rain. The pagoda tree in Worker Village had no sooner blossomed than its flowers flew away. Then, in a day, it seemed, summer descended with its battering sun to harden all it touched. Not even the nights were cool. At the clothesline, collecting laundry, the women grumbled and cursed. "The trees are bewitched," one of them said as Qing Yuan passed on his bicycle. The men came home exhausted, cursing like their women. The Revolution had begun the month before. In retrospect, Qing Yuan thought, the unforgiving seasons, their relentless onslaught, had been the Revolution's vanguard.

Mass rallies and public denunciations were now routine. *Dazibao* violated every surface. Arrests, both public and secret, had become commonplace. Destruction swept through the city. Homes were ransacked, and often even confiscated. Many of Qing Yuan's neighbors had already been taken away without explanation.

Loudspeakers, more of them, appeared at every corner. Bulletins blasted throughout the day, morning news, noon news, evening news, nightly news, and, in between, *special* news, their single purpose to justify and tout the imminent success of the Revolution. These broadcasts never failed, either, to warn the people about the class enemies secretly plotting around them. No one should take anything for granted. The enemy could be anyone.

"This morgue is the single haven from all this madness!" Lao Jia said one day, like he was telling a joke.

Qing Yuan laughed, yet remained as wary as he'd since grown. Superficially, their chats were as casual as they'd always been. Lao Jia, however, Qing Yuan sensed, had begun to choose his words with as much caution as had Qing Yuan himself. Neither wanted anything to do with the Revolution. Both knew that inasmuch as they wished or tried, their power amounted to that of children in a hurricane. The Revolution had devoured all in its path. They were in its eye, now, along with everyone else.

Depravity ruled. Tumult, riots, beatings, lootings, he saw them all daily, people vanishing, people dying, that this was worse than a war was his constant thought. Civilization, the ideal of it, anyway, had been contaminated. After a time, conscripted to the morgue, it had been difficult to imagine his life before the Revolution in '49. Now he couldn't imagine more than reaching his little hovel each morning after riding through a city whose every breath was an annihilating howl.

One morning after his shift, Qing Yuan walked into the mess hall of the canteen to find the benches and tables had vanished. Centered on a high wall loomed a massive portrait of Mao Zedong. Beneath it a crew of workers was building a platform. Construction materials were strewn about. At the top of a bamboo ladder a man was installing a loudspeaker—*another* loudspeaker. A stack of red slogan banners had been piled up nearby. Amidst the cacophony of shouting men, and of hammers and saws, the hospital employees in the long queue to the service window chattered and gawked. Qing Yuan saw Lao Jia squatting against a wall, smoking, his pail before him.

"What's happening here?"

Lao Jia swept out his arm like an impresario. "You can see it yourself, right?"

"Is this for some kind of conference?"

"Struggle session," Lao Jia said. "You know, the public humiliation and torture that's become the norm?"

"Today?"

"A lad in my dorm told me it will be tomorrow. Apparently the heads of the hospital have been purged. This session is for them."

Qing Yuan's legs had cramped up. He lowered his buttocks to the floor and reached for his toes. "It doesn't make sense."

"We're morgue keepers. Does anything we do make sense?" Lao Jia nodded toward to the queue. "You're not hungry?"

"I'll eat at Chow-Chow."

Lao Jia opened his pail. "Have some of mine. It's your meal ticket that paid for it."

"My legs hurt too much."

Lao Jia nudged Qing Yuan with an elbow. "How many?" he said.

"Twenty-one, nine of them suicides—two couples from coal gas poison, two drowned men, two women overdosed on sleeping pills, and a lad who rammed a pair of chopsticks into his throat."

"We are fucked," Lao Jia said. He looked Qing Yuan in the face. "Am I wrong?"

Qing Yuan reached again for his toes but couldn't touch more than his shins. Lao Jia fished a spoon from his pocket and began to eat. Qing Yuan rubbed his knees, then stood up.

"I have to go," he said, and Lao Jia waved his spoon at him.

He crossed the main road and turned down a narrow street lined with tumbledown shacks. Some had no windows, some had small openings for stove pipes, all of them roofed with tar paper or cheap canvas. From a large tree two street urchins dropped to the sidewalk beside Qing Yuan. They roared with laughter then fled down an alley in their broken shoes, spinning up puffs of smoke-like dirt.

Teenagers loitered everywhere, laughing, arguing, silent, half of them at least with the eyes of people who'd do anything for nothing on a moment's notice. On one of their dates—he and Feng Ge had been seeing each other quite a bit since that first day in the park— she told him her oldest daughter's school had closed. She went each day nonetheless, for propaganda work, she told Feng Ge. More than that, she had no notion as to her daughter's activities, a disturbing matter, she said. Qing Yuan scanned the kids he passed, half expecting to see Feng Ge's daughter smoking in the shade of a dusty tree.

Chow-Chow had set up at the back of an abandoned warehouse. The place served food from early morning to late at night, the one place within riding distance of Worker Village. An old couple ate at a corner table. Most of the other tables lay cluttered with dirty dishes.

Qing Yuan tiptoed over the food and grease to place his order at the service window. He watched the tired middle-aged waitress set her tub on a table and begin to fill it. She looked out the window, paused, then darted to the door.

"Fuck off, you stupid tramp," she shouted. "Come here again, and I'll break your other leg."

The tramp was FanFan. Evidently she had seen Qing Yuan enter the cafe and decided to wait for him. No sooner had he hung his pail over his handlebars than she appeared before him, her tattered bag dangling from her shoulder.

"Hello, sir." She was steeped in sweat and stunk like a bedpan full of waste.

Qing Yuan hadn't seen her for a time. She must have found more abundance in this neighborhood than in Worker Village. "Have you discovered some treasure here?" he said.

"I'm a tramp, sir," she said. "I go wherever my feet take me." Qing Yuan gestured at his pail, and her tin appeared like a weasel from a hole. "The streets never fail to entertain, right? Red Guards, parades, music, and news, so much, so much!"

"Do you still shelter at that school?" he said.

Fan Fan licked some sauce off her tin. "Thank you, sir." A fly landed on matted hair. She was faster than she looked. Her hand whipped up and killed the fly. "Feng Ge's husband died," she said.

"How do *you* know that?

"Everyone knew, at least in Worker Village," she said. "He used to talk with me and give me food," she said. "Like you."

"I heard he was killed in a fight," Qing Yuan said, hoping she'd tell him her version of the story.

But Fan Fan stared at her tin. "The noodles are still warm!" she said.

"I just got them." He mounted his bicycle. "Don't let them get cold, now," he said, and rode away.

11.

WHEN HE WENT IN for his shift, Qing Yuan found *dazibao*, in black letters on red and yellow and orange and blue paper, pasted on every wall. To his dismay, Lao Jia's name screamed from all of them. The place had been ransacked. The floors were dense with trash. He saw through the workstation window a man slouched in a chair, his face in his hands. No sooner had Qing Yuan appeared than the man leapt up as if the chair had been laced with barbs.

"Thank God you're here!" he said, gripping the edge of the desk. The man's swollen eyes told Qing Yuan he had been weeping for some time.

"Where's Lao Jia?" Qing Yuan said, and laid his bag on the desk.

"He . . . He . . . They took him," the man said, and glanced at the clock. "Three hours ago."

"*Took* him?"

"He was arrested," the man said.

Lao Jia's shirt hung on a peg. His dinner pail and chopsticks sat where they always did, on the storage cabinet. Qing Yuan shook the pail. Lao Jia's dinner was still in it. The lock on Lao Jia's drawer had been pried away. The drawer itself hung wide open, empty. Lao Jia had never trusted anyone in his dormitory. "They'd steal everything," he once told Qing Yuan, "even your underwear, if it served a purpose." He had always stored his money, ration card, meal tickets, and any important documents in the drawer at the morgue, never for a moment unlocked. He searched for Lao Jia's flask. Half a bottle of baijiu remained in the cabinet, but the flask was gone.

Qing Yuan looked at the man with real gravity. "Listen, brother," he said.

"Kong Jiu," the man said.

"Kong Jiu, please, tell me all you know."

"I've been cooped up here for three hours," he said, sobbing. "To watch these corpses. All these dead people! Awful!"

"But Lao Jia?"

Kong Jiu couldn't stop sobbing. He gripped the desk, his head bowed, tears and snot pouring from him. "He was outside when I arrived, fighting them, screaming and howling. They smashed him to the concrete and beat him to a pulp with clubs. Then they hogtied him and threw him in a truck. Even barely conscious he somehow managed to curse them as they bound him to a rail. Then they piled into the truck and sped away." Qing Yuan hadn't tried to interrupt Kong Jiu. "I wasn't alone, either," he said. "All kinds of people stood around, watching like children. Not one of us raised a hand."

"Do you think he's all right?" Qing Yuan said, and felt ridiculous.

"Does it sound like he was all right?"

Qing Yuan wanted to ask Kong Jiu where they'd taken his friend but knew it was pointless. In the hall by the door to the morgue, two corpses lay on gurneys.

Qing Yuan spun around and returned to the workstation, furious. "You left them on the gurneys!"

"I'm leaving," Kong Jiu said, chewing at his lip.

"You're working here now?"

"That's what I was told."

Qing Yuan studied this sad frail man. "Have I seen you before?"

"I am—I was—a nurse," Kong Jiu said as he shuffled off.

It took longer than Qing Yuan had thought to clean the corpses. He went to the toilet and let the water run over his head. He scrubbed and dried his face. He lit a cigarette and paced along the corridor gawping in disbelief at the *dazibao*.

"There's nothing we can do," he remembered Lao Jia saying, then thought of #19, also. The desire to learn her name had hounded him to no end, despite the improbability of his finding out.

The morgue became brighter as the night grew darker. He couldn't get clear of the thought that Lao Jia had been thrown into some dank room to bleed alone in the heat. Qing Yuan mopped the floor and cleaned the cabinets. He could smell the ghosts, a distinctive musky odor. If only they would call out to him. He tapped here and there, waiting for them to speak, as they did in his dreams, but received not a whisper. Sixteen years, he thought, and still here he was, sweating in the horrid coffin Lao Jia had once described as a piece of Ming furniture.

Qi Chu was an hour late. After a spell of smoking, Qing Yuan took Lao Jia's dinner pail from the cabinet and emptied it in the toilet. Another fifteen minutes passed before Qi Chu appeared.

"Has something happened to Lao Jia?"

"He was beaten and arrested."

"Fuck," Qi Chu said. "Were you here?"

"He was already gone."

"He always said this morgue was the single haven from the madness. And now look. It isn't true."

"There is no escape."

Qi Chu's eyes had glazed with fear. "I come from a peasant family. That makes me immune to all of this. Right?"

Qing Yuan laughed and walked away. He did not look at the *dazibao*. He'd nearly reached the door when Qi Chu called out.

"How many?" he said, but Qing Yuan didn't answer.

12.

It was one of those mornings when even breathing felt like labor. Qing Yuan dragged himself to the outpatient building, where he had arranged to meet Feng Ge and her daughter.

By now, he and Feng Ge could be said to have been dating. They'd gone so far as to shop at a department store. He'd bought fabric with his ration stamps that Feng Ge transformed into outfits for the children. A few days later, he found the young girl washing spinach at the tap, her baby brother by her side. Both were wearing new clothes. The boy had kept splashing water on his sister's face, and laughed and laughed every time she'd told him to stop. Qing Yuan couldn't help but notice her blighted hand.

He entered the lobby, walked straight to the gift store, and bought two tins of cookies, two of canned fruit, a bag of candy, and another of cupcakes.

"Someone is going to be very happy!" the clerk said.

In the lobby, behind the information desk, sat the cleaner who had delivered #19 to the morgue, scarfing food from his pail. The image of her body on the gurney, the stench of it, assailed Qing Yuan. He had done everything he could, he told himself. Then another part of him said that wasn't true. He had done nothing, absolutely nothing.

The cleaner gasped when he looked up to find Qing Yuan before him. A chunk of cabbage fell from his mouth.

"Breakfast or lunch?" Qing Yuan said.

"Both," the cleaner said, and swallowed hard. He hesitated for a moment, then closed his pail and slid over to make room on the bench for Qing Yuan. He sat beside the cleaner and offered him a cigarette. He took it and began to swab his teeth with a pinkie. "I was fucking starving," he said. "I've worked two shifts since yesterday—no dinner, no breakfast." He lit the cigarette and sucked on it hungrily.

"Remember that woman you sent me last month?" Qing Yuan said.

"The one picked up by a streetsweeper? Still breathing when I got her?"

"You wouldn't happen to know where they found her, would you?"

"The streetsweeper yelled at the emergency room. The security guard went out. I couldn't hear much more than something-something avenue."

"Victory Avenue?"

The cleaner shook his head. Qing Yuan understood. Anyone who'd experienced what the cleaner had, that night alone with #19, much less someone like himself, a man for whom death had become as common as rice, would be haunted to the end of their days. "Please don't tell me you still have her," the cleaner said.

"The police came and sent her to the crematorium."

"At least it's finished."

"No one came to bring her clothes. They took her away as a number. Number 19."

The two sat in silence, smoking, until Qing Yuan spotted Feng Ge and her daughter across the room. "I have to go," he said.

"I hope your day is better than mine," the cleaner said.

Feng Ge looked at the floor when Qing Yuan approached. "We're late, I know," she said. "I'm so sorry." The child stood gazing up at Qing Yuan with eyes that were as curious as they were sad. "You know Qing Yuan," Feng Ge said. "He's here to take care of you. Say hello."

Qing Yuan studied the girl's hands while she fidgeted. Their skin looked like freshly cut beets covered with yellowy blisters.

"This is for the kids," he said, and handed Feng Ge his bag of goodies.

"You're too generous," she said. "You can't possibly have enough ration stamps left for the month!"

"Please," he said, his face expanding at the thought of the joy his gift would fill the children with.

An hour later, Feng Ge and the girl came out of the treatment room. The bandages around her hands made them look like a pair of boxing gloves, Qing Yuan thought and suppressed his urge to laugh. The girl sat on a bench and swung her feet as she ate the candy. Qing Yuan couldn't say which made him happier, her treated hands or her pure delight. He touched her head and walked down the hall for the medicine the doctor had prescribed. The cashier gave him a ticket.

"How long will this take?"

"Your number will be called," the cashier said.

Qing Yuan looked at the ticket, stunned. The number on the ticket swam before him like germs under a microscope. He blinked repeatedly. He wanted to ask the cashier for another ticket, knowing it wouldn't matter. He'd been given this ticket, and on this ticket the number the woman had written was *#19*.

A tremor rushed through him—confusion, shame, self-loathing, vexation, rage. His mouth was dry, his hands cold. He was shaking, he realized. He felt he might collapse. This was fate from mythology. This could not be true. She was everywhere. She was haunting him, he thought. It was like he'd said to Qi Chu the other morning. *There is no escape.* But what was he supposed to do? Devote his life to learning her identity, to finding the villains who had slaughtered her? And then what? Avenge her? And then what after that? Avenge all the world? He could start in this awful city, right here, right now, and though he were immortal never finish the work.

He looked again at the ticket. He wanted to find he'd been delirious, hallucinating, dreaming, anything but the reality of this moment. The number, however, was the number—#19—nothing more, nothing less, a single number on an empty slip, #19, #19. Was this the doom Sister Wang had divined in his face? The *smack of doom*, she'd essentially said, was as much a part of his face as was his nose. Doom was nothing any of us could escape. Destiny, doom, fortune, fate, the name, the word, meant nothing before the thing itself. He'd paid for some medicine and received denunciation. No one could unknow what they knew. One could deny it, neglect it, ignore it, even for a time forget it, but never could one unknow it.

Feng Ge and her daughter were staring at him. He drew back his shoulders and raised his head. He smiled at the two, then he stuffed the ticket in his pocket and felt it like a scratching hand. Feng Ge knew that something was amiss. He willed his foot to move, and then the other behind it. How he reached the woman and the girl he could never explain.

"I want to see the fish," the child told her mother, and hopped away.

Indeed, a tank sat on a shelf across the room, its tiny fish drifting around their never-ending circle. The girl stood gazing into it, more toddler than heroic child. It was good to see her in this moment of innocence, Qing Yuan thought. For a moment he forgot his life. Feng Ge sat before him, stricken, like so many others, by atrocity while refusing to submit to it.

"Are you all right?" she said, her eyes brimming with concern.

"A thought came to me, a memory, actually. I'm sorry to have been so dramatic."

"It happens to all of us these days," she said. "It does to me, anyway. This life does whatever it wants."

He looked at her, then at the child before the tank. "Lao Jia was arrested," he said. "Yesterday evening." Feng Ge sighed. Her brow knit up. She smoothed a wrinkle on her pants. "I don't know where he is," Qing Yuan said.

"Even if you did, there's nothing you could do."

"It's so true, isn't it? This life does do whatever it wants. I wish I were brainless sometimes, a puppet. If we were brainless we could never feel that everything is wrong."

"You know I know, Qing Yuan," she said, and took his hand. "Nothing changes. It's never right."

Qing Yuan couldn't help himself. The ticket was wriggling in his pocket. "I'm sorry to bring this up. I've been thinking about it, I can't say why. It's just something I was wondering. I'm trying," he said, knowing the nincompoop he must have seemed, "to figure something out."

"Qing Yuan," she said. "Whatever it is, if I can help, I will."

"I'm sorry," he said again. "I'm really very sorry. It's just—

"Please."

"What day did your husband die? Or what day did they find him?"

She let go his hand. His stomach turned. She peered up, her eyes heavy with grief. He took back her hand and stroked her fingers as gently as he could, as though her hand were a newborn kitten.

"June 6th," she said, her voice no more than a satin whisper. "They found him early on June 6th."

Their eyes met in sorrow. Her fingers were quivering. He'd have done anything not to have asked such a hurtful thing. Yet he couldn't help himself. He had to know.

Feng Ge's husband and #19 had died on the same day, both of them murdered. His heart was pumping hard. The room had turned bright and hot. The roof could have been lifted away to let the sun pour down.

"And where?" he said, unable to stop. "Do you know where they found him?

"I thought I already told you everything I know."

"I know you did," he said, "but I forgot."

"The Red Guards sent his body to the morgue and called the police."

She looked at him, helpless. Her expression shifted minutely. He wasn't sure of anything now. He could have imagined it, he thought. But no. A faint shadow had crept over her, pulsing with wariness and fear. He wanted to say more. The words wouldn't come. Then the voice of the woman who had given him the ticket called out through a speaker. "#19 is ready," she said. Qing Yuan and Feng Ge stood as one and walked to the counter.

13.

A FEW DAYS LATER, near the end of his shift, two uniformed men appeared before Qing Yuan and without explanation ordered him to come with them. Qing Yuan asked why.

"Hurry up!" the first man barked.

Qing Yuan hadn't felt terrified for years, but now he was more afraid than ever. "I can't leave till my colleague comes to relieve me," he said.

"All right, all right," the other man said.

The men retreated to the corridor, scowling as they smoked. Qing Yuan opened the drawer with his name on it and set his watch on his employee card. He rolled a few bills in his handkerchief and slipped it into the front of his pants, beneath his underwear.

The men were watching him. They weren't about to let him shower, he knew, much less eat breakfast, sip some tea, smoke a cigarette. Nothing now seemed impossible.

He expected to see Qi Chu soon enough, but instead, the manager, whom he almost never saw, appeared with a skinny young man wearing a Red Guard armband and the ubiquitous green cap. They spoke for a moment with the men in the corridor. Then, in a voice utterly flat the Red Guard ordered Qing Yuan to open his drawer and the cabinet. The guard scrabbled through each, the veins on his thin hands like twine. He left the drawer and cabinet open and walked away without a word.

"Lock the drawer and give me the key," the manager said without looking at Qing Yuan.

The men led him to an old green truck, the canopy over its bed fashioned from canvas and wood. Four men were already in it. They stunk as badly as Qing Yuan himself.

"Hurry up," the driver said as the guards squeezed into the cab. Qing Yuan sat on one of two long benches, and the truck lurched away.

The city rolled out behind him, its streets a scroll of horse-driven wagons and trash carts and buses and rickety bicycles and an ever-growing mob of workers trudging toward their destinations. A donkey cart loaded with cabbage was blocking a bus, its driver honking as he cursed. The farmer lashed his donkey with a stick, and the donkey reared up and howled. A swarm of factory women, some bearing infants, bickered and snapped as they waited for the bus. The truck moved off to the screeching of babies and women.

This day was no different than the last, and yet Qing Yuan knew very well that things had fundamentally changed. He had been arrested. All along his fate had been waiting, just here, for him to reach it. Life does whatever it wants, he thought.

But for the breakfast stalls, each with a queue snaking down the walks, most of the shops were still shuttered. It had been ten hours since his last meal. The smell of fried dough was unbearably enticing. The impulse to leap out struck him—he still had his money—but knew he'd be caught and thrashed.

Lao Jia hadn't eaten before his arrest, either, he thought, and imagined his friend's battered face. They had shared everything, down to a fate neither of them had imagined. How could he have believed it would be different for them?

The truck rattled on, stopping several times to arrest more people. Some looked out blankly at the street. Others hugged their knees. The heat was overwhelming. The stench was sickening. No one said a word.

Qing Yuan counted the faces around him. First it was twenty-one, then twenty, then twenty-one again. Eighteen of his fellows were men and three were women, all of them middle-aged. The women wore white doctor's coats and caps and smelled of the same antiseptic that poisoned the air of the morgue. The truck was full, and yet the guards shoved in another woman maybe fifty-five years old, furiously gasping. The truck lurched on before she could sit. She toppled into some men opposite Qing Yuan. Several of them insulted her. One simply laughed.

Despite her cap, Qing Yuan could see her head had been shaved to the skin. She was the director of the dermatology department at his hospital, Qing Yuan realized. He held onto the rail and gave her his hand while asking one of the men who'd cursed her to make a little room. She sat beside him, her neck, he noticed, ringed with bruises fresh and old.

"I work in the morgue at your hospital," he said.

"What can the Revolution want with a morgue keeper?" she said. Qing Yuan felt the blood rushing to his face. He was furious, not for having been kind to the woman, but for the words she had used to describe him—"morgue keeper." He felt he'd been slapped in the face. After a moment, her voice softer, the woman said, "I take it this is your first time."

Qing Yuan nodded. "And you?"

"Why haven't I seen you at the struggle sessions?"

"I work the night shift."

"I don't often deal with the morgue. My patients may suffer, but typically they don't die."

"People with skin problems don't die?"

"Psoriasis, for example. There is no cure. People who've been cursed with it are likely to suffer before they die, but, still, it takes a long time."

They passed through a quarter with dilapidated houses and small broken shops. The dermatologist clung to Qing Yuan's arm as the truck lurched and bounced. She must have noticed Qing Yuan sniffing the air, heavy with the smell of coal and grease.

"They're going to starve us, you know."

They passed through an enormous gate then stopped at the edge of a field two hundred meters long at least, filled to capacity with people. No sooner had he and his fellow prisoners debouched from the truck than they were surrounded by Red Guards, each with a coin-sized metal badge depicting Mao Zedong pinned to their chests. The young man who had collected Qing Yuan bawled out commands. The other guards called him "Captain."

The prisoners were told to remove their shoes and drape them from their necks by the laces. Then they were ordered to form a line. A guard with short wooden boards on which information about the prisoners had been written went down the line and hung the boards over their shoes.

Qing Yuan's board announced that he was an "Active Counterrevolutionary." His name had been scribbled onto the board with red ink. The shoes and the board were heavy. The laces and rough twine bit into his neck. He stood burning in the heat as he understood the source of the bruises on the dermatologist's neck. A martial song blasted from speakers around the field. The mass of people were singing.

Flanked by Red Guards, Qing Yuan and his fellows were marched up a stairway leading to a stage. A frail old man lost his balance and toppled backward into Qing Yuan. They tumbled off the stairs onto the concrete slab below. Several guards rushed in screaming and kicked them repeatedly before dragging them to the stage.

Blood poured from a gash on the old man's face. The guards forced the prisoners to line up across the stage with their heads bowed and arms aloft. A rank of police stood close behind.

Yawning before them stretched a crowd beyond count. Qing Yuan couldn't discern one person from the next. There were only maniacal faces beneath waving red books and portraits of Mao Zedong. In every direction swayed huge red banners. A single unified voice sang to the music blaring from the ubiquitous speakers.

Soon the music stopped, and a terrible voice roared out. "The struggle session will begin with a rendition of 'The East is Red.'" The crowd thundered its applause. A lone woman began to sing through the speakers, and the people joined in.

> *The east is red, the sun is rising.*
> *From China comes Mao Zedong!*
> *He strives for the people's happiness,*
> *Hurrah, he is the people's greatest savior!*

The sun battered down. The crowd was delirious. The song went on and on. The savagery in the eyes of the people before Qing Yuan was terrifying. He wondered how he could have buckled with such meekness to these people and their brutality, how he could have gone on pretending in the face of so much poverty and death that he himself would never know it? Why hadn't he raged? Why had he not rebelled? One evil man, he thought, a single evil man, had reduced him and his millions of fellows to creatures who existed to be crushed.

His vision had contracted to a point before his feet. He could no longer see the massed people, but only hear their voices spitting their hatred and wrath. Nothing about the prisoners was theirs anymore. Not even their names were their own. Everything about them—what they did, where they had come from, their family histories, their relatives—the whole of it had been manipulated into objects of incomprehensible malice. The terrible voice spewed one accusation after another. With each new slander, the mob grew increasingly rabid. Massed as one, these so-called people had great power. Alone, like him, they were impotent as dust.

He could no longer hold himself up. He bent with his hands on his knees, lower and lower, until he was looking through his legs at the scene behind him. The identical uniforms, the identical legs and shoes, the identical rifles of the police behind him, the identical way they stood on the concrete, all of it upside-down, seemed like some terrible hallucination. Sweat streamed down his face and fell in drops between his feet. He felt at any moment he would faint or, worse, soil himself. He hadn't been to the toilet for hours. If only he could sit down, if only they would give him two drops of water and let him drift to sleep.

He heard the terrible voice say his father's name, and then his own. The voice pulsed with hatred as it began to catalogue his father's alleged crimes. Qing Yuan had heard these slurs many times, and yet even after all these years they stung with a freshness he couldn't have fathomed. His father had been denounced as a villain and an enemy of the State and then summarily executed. Now, by association, Qing Yuan was a villain, too, *an active coun-terrevolutionary*, the terrible voice said. As the litany of crimes went on, Qing Yuan felt himself collapsing, his past on the one hand and this moment on the other battling to wipe him out.

His father indeed had refused to give up his gold. It had seemed wise at the time. Never in Qing Yuan's maddest visions could he have foreseen the effects of that decision, how far and wide they'd ripple. His father had been murdered, his mother perished of grief, all they'd had robbed by the State. Qing Yuan had then been forced into the work of a man who night after night cleaned the bodies of the dead, so many of whom had been mutilated in ways too terrible to speak. Sixteen years on, here it all was, again, bearing down on him in the form of this terrible voice shrieking to the fanatics before him. He was powerless, he knew. He was no longer even a man, he thought. He was no longer even human.

He closed his eyes and thought of his father, his dashing intel-ligent father, sharing the philosophy of his art. "Divinely exquisite when using gold, daringly striking when using silver—that's the secret, my son." At the banquet to celebrate Qing Yuan's gradua-tion from university, his father had fixed him with his gold–black eyes. "I know you've had other thoughts," he'd said, "but really you should consider joining my business. It would all be yours before long, you know. I want to spend more time with your mother. With your taste, your instinct for beauty, and my knowledge and experience? You would be astonished!"

Father! You still give me strength! I won't die here, I promise!

The platform seemed to be giving way. A pit opened up beneath him. He felt himself plummeting, and then he felt nothing. He didn't know how long he'd been out. He swam back into consciousness to Red Guards kicking him while the mob roared with approval.

"Beat him! Beat him harder! He's faking! He's shaming us all! Beat him! Beat him!"

The blows rained down. A fist crashed against his ear. A moment later, he couldn't hear more than a droning buzz.

14.

HE AWAKENED TO AN IMPENETRABLE DARKNESS, HIS SHOES still around his neck. Hard lumps bore into his back. He lifted a hand to his face but couldn't see it. His legs were numb. His whole body was numb. He had wet himself, but didn't know it until he put his hand on his lap. Mildew, feces, urine, sweat—wherever they had put him, the place was rank with these odors, along with others, the scent of coal, maybe, he thought, mixed, he couldn't really say, with rotting wood.

From the floor above he heard stomping feet and scraping chairs. A woman was shouting, and then a man. He realized he was hearing these things with only one ear. He put his finger into the bad ear and jiggered it, to no avail. He recalled the blow he'd taken on the stage as he was being beaten. In all likelihood, he thought, he was now half deaf.

When it grew quiet again, Qing Yuan discerned the breathing of people about him. He pushed himself up and took the shoes from his neck. He reached down his pants for his handkerchief. It and the bills it had held were gone. He strained to see anything, but the greater he struggled the darker the room seemed to grow.

"Who are you?" a woman said.

"I'm a morgue keeper," he said.

"I am a gynecologist," she said, as if introducing herself to an audience. "Hello?" she said. No one responded. "I know you're here," she said.

One by one his fellows began to announce themselves, a lab director, a pediatrician, a surgeon.

"Is that everyone?" the gynecologist said. No one replied.

"Does anyone know where we are?" Qing Yuan said.

"This," the lab director said, "is the Provincial Medical University."

"I saw no sign at the entrance."

"It was destroyed when the Red Guards made it their headquarters."

"But *this* place," Qing Yuan said. "What is it?"

"A coal room," the lab director said.

"Five prisoners in a coal room," the gynecologist said.

"We are not prisoners," the surgeon said.

"Certainly we've been arrested," the pediatrician said. "That makes us prisoners. Even if only for now."

"We were brought here for a struggle session," the surgeon said. "That's different."

"The struggle session is over," the lab director said.

"I listened to every speech," the surgeon said, "and didn't hear a word about an arrest."

The gynecologist sighed. "This is most definitely an arrest. They did the same to my husband. He was taken two weeks ago, and I haven't seen or heard from him since. I went to his department. No one knew a thing."

"They would have needed a warrant," the pediatrician said.

"Quite right," the surgeon said. "I studied law for two years before switching to medicine. I know the procedure. They can't arrest anyone without a warrant."

"All of that supposes a legal system," the lab director said. "What if there's no such thing anymore?"

"Nonsense!" the surgeon said. "Utter nonsense! It's not an arrest till I see a warrant."

"Where is your law, now?" the gynecologist said. "Where is your righteous court?

"This is illegal. We have the right to—"

"We have nothing," the lab director said. "No rights, no law, nothing!"

"The Party could never wrong a good person," the surgeon said.

"Then you must be very bad," the pediatrician said.

Qing Yuan could no longer restrain himself. "We were taken from our places of work. We were denounced before a mob of thousands. We were viciously beaten. We're all bad people, all of us, very, very bad."

"I am indeed a good person," the surgeon squealed, "and I believe in the Party!"

"What you are," the pediatrician said, "is crazy."

"The Revolution has just begun," the surgeon said. "Misinterpretations and confusion are entirely understandable. Every error will soon be corrected!"

Someone's bowels croaked, and soon the air reeked of human gas. For a long while, no one spoke. There was only darkness, and heat, the awful stench, the sound of strained breathing, the occasional sigh, the clearing of a throat.

"I have two little ones," the gynecologist said at last. "A son of seven and a daughter of nine. How can they survive without me?"

"Children are hardier than adults," the pediatrician said. "I once had three patients with measles, five, seven, and nine years old. They all lived by themselves. Their parents? Suicide! The nine-year-old became a rag-picker. She raised her siblings on her own. Of course, they struggled, but such courage is—"

"My daughter is not a rag-picker!" the gynecologist cried.

"That's not what I'm saying," the pediatrician said. "If one falls into a pond, one must never imagine they'll drown but hope they might catch a fish."

"How dare you patronize me!" the gynecologist said, sobbing.

"I'm sorry," the pediatrician said. "But I do believe your children will be fine. We'll all be home soon, tomorrow, if not today!"

"Even if they do let us out," the lab director said, "we might not have our jobs anymore."

"I can always babysit for friends or neighbors," the pediatrician said. "I'm a good storyteller, too. I make people laugh." He paused for a moment, as if deliberating. "But surely one of us here won't lose his job," he said. "We always need someone to care for the dead. Am I right, Comrade Morgue Keeper?"

"We can all be morgue keepers," Qing Yuan said, thinking of Lao Jia and how he had once said, "When you tend the dead, you leave the weight of your own life behind and see the truth of everything."

The room grew quiet, the darkness heavier. There was only the sound of the gynecologist weeping.

"What they said about me were lies!" she sobbed. "Nothing they said was true!"

"Is there something you're trying to prove?" the surgeon said.

"I renounced my parents and my family when they fled to America! I have delivered thousands of babies and never lost one—not one! I've volunteered to work in the villages in Guizhou, training doctors and delivering babies for peasants. Seven years in the mountains, with no running water, no electricity! How could I possibly be considered a reactionary? It's madness, I tell you, madness!"

Qing Yuan could smell her sour breath. His eyes ached trying to see her.

"I toiled in the countryside myself," the surgeon said, "right after college. For five years I collected herbs from the villagers, door to door, year after year—exhausting work, believe me! It was an honor, I felt. It was my contribution to the nation."

"Are you a Party member?" the pediatrician said.

"A ridiculous question, Comrade."

"I'm assuming, then, that you're enjoying the benefits the Party has bestowed upon you," the pediatrician said.

"To hell with you!" the surgeon shouted. "My wife and I live with her parents, and we have nothing, but I am very, very proud!"

"I'm afraid to inform you, Comrade Surgeon," the pediatrician said, "that if I go to hell, you're coming with me."

The coal bit into Qing Yuan. He wriggled to ease his discomfort and leaned his head against the wall. He closed his eyes and tried to imagine Feng Ge's face. He thought about her helpless smile when in the hospital lobby he had questioned her about her husband's death. That smile, along with the pain and fear in her eyes, had haunted him ever since. How warm and tremulous her hand had felt in his. They had talked about meeting this Saturday for an early dinner. His temples throbbed at the thought of her waiting alone outside the restaurant. How would she feel when she learned of his arrest? He could imagine the rumors she'd soon hear, the whispers of his capture, the accusations that would follow. How could he explain any of this? No reason would suffice. His hands and legs began to tremble. It felt as though even the fetid air was trembling.

"There must be some impossible mistake in my dossier," the surgeon said. It sounded to Qing Yuan as though the surgeon was inconsolably ashamed, as if he'd struck a cat on his bicycle in the dark.

"You know very well," the lab director said, "they can write whatever they like in our dossiers. 'To be kept into perpetuity.' That's what's on the first page of every last one, in big red letters. How else do you think we got here?"

"Has anyone considered," the gynecologist said, "just how bizarre it is that they have a dossier for each of us—each and every one of us, in the millions! They know everything about us! Like he just said, if they don't know what they want or need, they make it up! Someone could be standing outside the door of this hellhole this very instant, you know. They could be writing down every word we say, word for word and then some, every tittle of which they'll use against us the instant we stop talking long enough for them to understand what we ourselves already know."

"We're damned if we do," the lab director said, "and damned if we don't, as they say."

"A tragicomedy," Qing Yuan said.

"What's that?" the surgeon said.

"Like *The Book of Job*," Qing Yuan said. "Or poor little Kafka. You know. Our predicament really is quite absurd."

"Easy enough to say," the pediatrician said. "I doubt, however, that for you, our valiant *morgue keeper*, a dossier even exists."

"Precisely," the lab director said to Qing Yuan. "What could the State possibly want with you?"

"Have you considered *why* I'm a morgue keeper?" Qing Yuan said. He wanted to see these people. Their voices in this rank blackness were more frightening than those of the ghosts in the morgue. He could brush away the twigs in their hair. He could lay a hand on their shoulders and grace them with his smile. They would be people again, suffering as he was suffering. They would see each other and know the meaning of what they shared.

"What?" the surgeon said.

"What child tells his parents, 'Mommy, Daddy, when I grow up I want to be a morgue keeper'?" Qing Yuan said.

"You're boring us," the pediatrician said. "Get to the point."

"It is a worthy question," the gynecologist said.

"It was my father," Qing Yuan said. "He owned a jewelry business until 1949. In a single night they took my family and everything we had. Before they came, my father had hidden a small amount of gold in the floor. Our family steward betrayed us. Then *they* appeared and took my father away. The next day he was executed as an enemy of the State. My mother died a few weeks later."

Qing Yuan hadn't realized until now that a swarm of mosquitoes had enveloped him. He'd been slapping at them all this time. When he had first returned to consciousness and understood where he was, he could feel nothing. His entire body was numb, and one of his ears was deaf. Only now had he begun to feel again. His whole body seemed to be roasting in flames. Everyone else was slapping at themselves, as well. The shrill whine of the mosquitoes had been so incessant as to seem the silence itself. There had to be water in this place, he thought, somewhere, a disgusting fetid bucket or pool of hidden water. The mosquitoes were factually a multitude. And it was as if they'd been waiting years for this moment, days and days of hunger suffered knowing they'd be rewarded for their patience with an everlasting feast.

"And that's when they put you in the morgue," the lab director said.

"After my recantation."

"You denounced your father, too?" the gynecologist said. She sounded shocked.

"Damn these mosquitoes!" the pediatrician said, slapping at himself.

"Maybe the coal will help," the surgeon said. "Rub it on your face."

"It won't," the pediatrician said. "I've tried."

"It's always the same after a denunciation," the lab director said. "You're forced into the most menial job."

"But what about, you know, *before*?" the gynecologist said to Qing Yuan, her voice softer now.

"I studied literature and art. Then I studied jewelry with my father. I was going take his business when he retired."

"I tried to speak the truth when they took me in '57," the pediatrician said.

"But they released you," the surgeon said. "Didn't they? After you told them the *truth*?"

"Ha!" the pediatrician said. "They kept me under lights, day and night, for two whole months! They starved me for days. Then they gave me salty food without any water. They beat me almost daily with a hose. And then without explanation, one day they sent me on my way."

"What a fantasy, what a dream," the surgeon said. "You must have the magic power of the Monkey King."

"We are *bad*," the pediatrician said, "and this darkness is but an appetizer before a disgusting meal. They are going to feed us the finest shit the world has ever known."

"I need the toilet," the lab director said.

"Can anyone find the door?" the gynecologist said.

The surgeon hammered on the wall with his fist. "Please," he shouted, "open the door! We need the toilet! Please!"

They heard footsteps and coarse laughter, but the door remained shut.

"This is a coal room," Qing Yuan said. "And anyway, haven't you noticed the stench? This won't be the first time someone has relieved themselves in here."

They heard the lab director unbuttoning his trousers, and then the splattering of his urine.

"Forgive me," he said.

"God is always fair," the pediatrician said.

"God," the surgeon said, and snickered, "is dead. Where have you been, anyway, Comrade?

"That is the logic of a school child," the pediatrician said. "Just because you can't see it doesn't mean it's not there. The arrogance of the atheist has never ceased to astound me." No one spoke. Qing Yuan heard one of his fellows scraping on the wall with a chunk of coal. Qing Yuan felt his face. It was lumpy with what felt like hives. The mosquitoes were relentless. There was no escape. "The ingenuity of humans is a tragic paradox," the pediatrician said, "in precise opposition to the way of things. Shiva destroyed so that she might create. We, on the other hand, create so that we might destroy. Thankfully, all things that fail to work with the way of things ultimately transform into things that do. That is the way. We are here for a blip. Our imprisonment is an illusion. This is all a dream."

Qing Yuan and the lab director laughed. Qing Yuan hadn't thought of things that way, but knew the pediatrician was right the moment he heard his words. He thought the gynecologist had chortled with them. But actually she had whimpered. Qing Yuan felt her next to him, her body in spasms.

"Don't any of you even dare to think I will relieve myself in front of you," she said, and slapped at a mosquito. "I won't," she cried, "I won't!"

Qing Yuan slapped at yet another mosquito, too. Everyone was slapping themselves. It was as if they were applauding a fantastic theater act. There was little left to them but salty skin, he thought, knowing the mosquitoes would go on taking from them until nothing but bones remained.

15.

Soon, beyond the wall, they heard shuffling feet and chopsticks drumming on tins, filth-screeching boys and jabbering girls. Keys rattled at the door, and then it creaked open and a beam of light jerked from face to face. There in the doorway loomed the captain, a flashlight in one hand, a club in another. "Up, now, and move!" he said.

Qing Yuan seemed to have been cloven in two. The pain in his back and haunches, the blows he had endured at the hands of the Red Guards, every muscle screamed in protest as he moved. He put on his shoes then stood with a groan and sagged against the wall. The captain jumped over, snapping. "Move!" he said, and swung his club with brutal precision. Qing Yuan wailed as he felt the crack on his shoulder. The pediatrician tottered forward and took Qing Yuan by an arm.

Together they stumbled through the door. The pediatrician was a heavy set man with a gray beard and glittering teeth. His broad face was streaked with grime, but his grip was warm and firm. As Qing Yuan looked into his eyes—mirthful and intelligent despite their predicament—he detected an impossible tenderness.

The surgeon stood apart from the group. From the holes in his socks his crooked toes peeked out like the snouts of shrews. He stared at them with a look of detached surprise, as if this were the first time he had seen them. To Qing Yuan's left stood the gynecologist, a petite middle-aged woman. Her shoulder-length hair was matted with sweat and dust, and her skin was crimson with sunburn. Two of the buttons on her soiled white shirt were missing. She must have sensed Qing Yuan's gaze. She looked at him with a vague smile.

The lab director exchanged a glance with Qing Yuan, too, then slouched against the wall. Qing Yuan had seen many terrible faces, but he was as appalled at this one as he was saddened. The lab director's face was a comprehensive scowl he had to have worn for so long, for many years at least, that it was marred with deep wrinkles and lines. A small thick scar ran from a temple to an eye. Though the eye had been but slightly disfigured, it nevertheless imbued the man's face with a somewhat villainous effect. His thick hair, moreover, was solid white. The man, Qing Yuan surmised, must have been brooding since childhood.

Qing Yuan touched the lab director's shoulder, but he shrugged him off. The air out here was stale, too, though nothing like that of the coal room. Here at least they could breathe. They were ordered to stand in a row with their eyes fixed on the ground.

The captain, surrounded by a crowd of mean-eyed teenagers, stood with one hand on his hip. "Toilet first," he shouted, "food afterward! Understand?" When none of the prisoners spoke, he struck the wall with his club hard enough to dent the plaster. "Answer!"

"Yes!" they shouted as one.

"Captain," a teenage girl said. "These eggs are more rotten than most. They are very bad and actually stink!"

"One of them wet his pants," a young boy said, sniggering.

"That's nothing!" the girl said. "We're going to make them shit their pants!"

Qing Yuan was let into the toilet. A square window faced the door, its shattered glass strewn across the floor. A faint draft ran over him, an unexpected relief. On the floor lay a squatting pan, and beside it was a broken bamboo basket overflowing with soiled toilet paper. From one of the brick walls a concrete trough cantilevered out. A single tap on a rusty pipe hung above it. He went to the trough and removed his shoes and socks. Then he stripped off his clothes and draped them over the trough.

"What are you doing?" the pediatrician said from the pit he was squatting over.

Qing Yuan opened the tap. The pipe groaned as a stream of murky water rushed out. He cupped his hands and splashed the water over his body. The chill seeped into his aching muscles. For a moment the pain vanished. He soaked his clothes then scrubbed and wrung them out. He leaned in and, despite the water's rustiness, gulped down as much as he could take.

"You'll make yourself sick," the pediatrician said.

Qing Yuan dressed in his sopping clothes and stumbled to the pit to relieve himself.

Once they'd been wrangled back to the hall, they were ordered to sit on the floor, legs crossed. A gang of teenagers appeared with trays of food—a tin of porridge and a fist-sized chunk of cornbread for each prisoner.

The gynecologist sipped the porridge. "Too salty!"

She removed her glasses and rubbed her eyes with the knuckles of her fingers. Qing Yuan took a bite of the cornbread. It was dry and coarse, the worst thing he'd ever put in his mouth. To help him swallow, he sipped the porridge, which, as the gynecologist had complained, tasted more like salt than anything else.

The lab director must not have eaten for days. Qing Yuan looked away for a moment, and when he looked back, the man's food had vanished. The pediatrician hadn't finished. He chewed each mouthful like a man sedated. It seemed he was purposefully refusing to swallow, as if to do so he might lose some gift he had been told was priceless. After a time he began to wheeze, even as he showed no sign of discomfort. Then, finally, with his last bit of bread, he mopped up the remaining driblets of porridge, placed the wad on his tongue, and sucked on it without chewing until it had dissolved away. Qing Yuan put down his half-empty tin and belched. No one said a word.

The teenagers retrieved the tins. The Red Guards accompanied the group to the toilet once more, where they all gulped as much of the filthy water as they could.

"When we put you back," the captain said, "do not speak. If we hear even one of you, you will all be punished. Now consider your guilt. Think of how you'll repent!"

"Not a chopstick, not even a spoon!" the surgeon whispered, once the door had clanged shut.

"A lad was sent to me weeks ago," Qing Yuan whispered. "He had punctured his throat with a pair of chopsticks."

"We could kill each other," the lab director whispered.

"Suicides are despicable," the surgeon whispered.

"We won't have to," the pediatrician whispered, "so long as we're at the mercy of these vicious devils."

"Civilization collapsed long before this revolution," the lab director whispered.

"Civilization?" the pediatrician whispered. "When will you stop using such meaningless words?"

"How could anyone have raised someone like the captain?" the gynecologist whispered.

"Some of these insane children were simply born that way," the lab director whispered. "In my opinion, they should be euthanized the moment they're diagnosed as such."

Qing Yuan felt that he'd become little more than a spectator in this relentless black, as impotent as he was invisible. A vision gathered, of #19 in the distance, gliding slowly toward him, shrouded in a bloody sheet. A faint breeze bore her stench to him. As she drew near, she spread her arms to reveal her body and face. Her body was as horrifying as when Qing Yuan had first seen her, but her face hadn't been touched. It was a plain face, framed by two long braids, her nose too flat and eyes too close and small. A number of moles spoiled her features. Her mouth, however, was sumptuous. Something about it seemed to transform the rest of her face, as by a spell, into something mysteriously alluring. She gazed into Qing Yuan's eyes, not with malevolence but with gratitude and compassion. Without looking away, her expression unmoved, she swept a hand from her chest to her belly, as if to say, *Behold, see what the world has done.* Her stench had vanished. The air smelled fresh, like a meadow in spring. #19 dropped her sheet and stood before him naked in her gore, then, as slowly as she had approached, passed behind him. He turned on his haunches to watch her vanish in the dark.

Throughout this vision, Qing Yuan had known he was a prisoner with four other prisoners. Now that #19 had gone her way, the sense of his body returned. He had been beaten then thrown onto a pile of waste and coal to be devoured by mosquitoes that had propagated exponentially in what had to be the scummiest of water. This was reality. This was the fact.

How he had been driven by anguish and despair and often too much rage as he scoured the city in search of even the meanest scrap of information, anything at all about a missing woman, a *murdered* woman. How he had been driven through the fog of death that tainted the whole of life itself, that smothered every motion and breath beneath the summer's unforgiving sun. How he had been driven by guilt and shame, alone in the morgue in the belly of night, to clean a never-ending procession of corpses. He had been driven and driven without ever knowing how. He was still being driven. He would be, he felt, driven for what remained of his days.

Yet in spite of everything, his endless suffering, the endless suffering, likely, of every person he laid eyes on—it comforted him a little to know he wasn't alone—he regretted not an instant of his pursuit for answers about #19. A man was capable of anything, good or bad, he had always believed. This was why he had told #19 that he would learn who had harmed her and why. He had found the strength to accept his life and to carry on. Now, here in this wretched blackness, his convictions began to crumble.

What would happen, he thought, if he died here in this place? The clothes he wore now would be the clothes in which he'd be burned. Or the Red Guards could strip him naked for fun, as some villain had stripped #19. Like her, he'd be sent to the crematorium, an anonymous man with a tag around a stiffened toe. By the time Feng Ge or perhaps Lao Jia—if he himself was still alive, Qing Yuan thought—heard of his death, he'd have been reduced to a bowl of ashes. He considered further and understood with cheer that in the grime of this endless madness there remained an immaculate jewel. He—no longer the "he" he'd believed himself to be until then—would at last behold the cosmos. The cosmos, yes, the long-awaited cosmos!

Eight other hands beat out an arrhythmic tattoo in the darkness, the slap!-slap! of swatting on skin. It disturbed him more than the buzzing of the mosquitoes itself. Now and then a hiss or a groan accentuated the cadence in dreadful counterpoint.

The men had shrugged off their dignity. Having drunk so much water, they stood to relieve themselves without comment or apology. The splatter of their urine on the coal was plain. The little room grew increasingly pungent with the urine's fresh acridity layered over the hardened reek of moldering waste from the countless prisoners that had come before. They had stopped speaking. In time, the constant slapping abated, as well. Their energy had abandoned them. They had little but the vestiges of their hope. More than the incessant drone of mosquitoes and the occasional futile thwap, Qing Yuan heard but the ragged breathing of his fellows, each of them lost in their private misery.

"I have a sunburn," the gynecologist whispered, "so I shouldn't scratch."

For a while now she had remained slumped beside Qing Yuan, groaning. Her sour breath came and went. He said nothing but reached out to console her with a touch on her shoulder.

"That porridge was too salty," she whispered. "I shouldn't have drunk all that water." She pushed herself up and stumbled to a corner. "I'm so sorry." Qing Yuan heard the rustle of her clothes, followed by the hiss from between her legs. She sobbed like a child as she pleaded with the men. "I'm so sorry, I'm so very sorry."

Soon they heard clinking keys. The door opened to reveal two Red Guards in silhouette. Even the gloomy light from the hall was blinding. Qing Yuan raised an arm against it. A man stepped in and without a word dragged the surgeon away. The other man slammed the door.

"An interrogation," the lab director whispered.

"They call it 'midnight snacks,'" the pediatrician whispered.

About an hour later, they came for the lab director. Qing Yuan heard the footsteps down the hall. Doors opened and closed, and chair legs scraped on the floor overhead. The muffled shouts and the banging became indistinguishable.

When the lab director returned some hours later, it seemed to Qing Yuan that the light through the doorway was brighter. Morning had come, he knew.

"Are you all right?" the gynecologist whispered.

"Yes," the lab director whispered. "I repented."

"It can't be quite that simple," the pediatrician whispered.

"Repentance means nothing," the lab director whispered. "I know that. They've already condemned me."

"*Who* we are no longer matters," the pediatrician whispered. "We are who they say we are."

Communism answers for everything, Qing Yuan thought, and remembered Lao Jia. "My friend always sang 'The Internationale' while cleaning the corpses," he whispered. "It was his way of saying goodbye to the dead." Everyone quietly laughed.

"*That* is not funny!" the pediatrician whispered. No one spoke, no one moved.

"In a few short years," the lab director said, "we have been turned from thinking beings into vicious animals."

"Speak for yourself," the gynecologist whispered. "I care for babies and mothers."

Qing Yuan imagined the woman in her white coat and cap, beside a mother cradling her newborn child. Then he thought of the dead babies flung onto the hospital fires and wondered if the gynecologist knew their fate.

"You said we would be going home soon?" the gynecologist whispered.

"Well, we're not," Qing Yuan whispered.

"I will only win," the lab director whispered, "if I can destroy a villain."

The door opened again, and the captain ordered them all down a path that led to a sand pit. Qing Yuan had been blind until now, but here, cast all at once into the blasting sun, his world transformed into a stabbing yellow glare through which swirled nebulous figures and shapes. Yet another song for the Revolution was wailing from the loudspeakers. He'd only just realized where he was before he and his fellows were shoved into the pit and commanded by a voice to kneel.

"I don't kneel, I won't kneel, I never kneel!" the gynecologist screamed. She was still beside Qing Yuan, pitching and writhing. "I won't!" she cried. "I won't, I won't, I won't!"

"You will," the captain said, "and you will do it till I say otherwise!"

A Red Guard, no more than a young teenager, appeared from the haze of yellow to kick the backs of her knees, and she collapsed face down into the sand. The boy stepped on her calf and dragged her up until she was indeed kneeling.

Qing Yuan thought they were about to be shot. Why else would they have been driven to this pit and made to kneel?

"Listen!" the captain said, and retreated to the shade of a nearby tree under which Qing Yuan could faintly make out a number of Red Guards in chairs smoking cigarettes.

Without warning, the terrible song was cut short and a monotonous voice from the speakers began to report the news.

Waves of heat shimmered above the burning sand. The

pediatrician had slouched on the side of the pit with his chin on his chest. His face was streaked with coal and sweat. His eyes were closed, but his mouth hung open as if trying to speak. The gynecologist panted miserably. Her hands were caked with grime, gripping her soiled pants. Her face and neck were riddled with mosquito bites.

The lab director had been made to kneel on Qing Yuan's other side. His face was swollen and bruised.

"They beat you," Qing Yuan whispered.

The lab director ignored this and nodded toward the captain with his guards in the shade.

"Those little monsters over there. But the captain is the worst, a bastard of the lowest sort."

"We heard him barking last night," Qing Yuan said.

"Just wait till you feel his bite. They beat the surgeon for God knows how long. I heard him screaming all night in the next room over. When I saw him in the toilet this morning, he was peeing his pants because he couldn't unbutton them. His hands were the size of eggplants." Qing Yuan could only gasp. "They smashed them with a hammer."

Merely to look at the Red Guards nauseated Qing Yuan. None of them seemed older than seventeen. The captain couldn't have been older than twenty. That they could do to the surgeon what the lab director had described, much less that they could imagine doing it, when they should have been studying and dating, seemed to Qing Yuan something more like the hallucinations of a lunatic.

"How old do you think the captain might be?" he said.

"Nineteen years and two months," the lab director said. "He was a freshman at the university."

"How do you know?" Qing Yuan said, and wiped the sweat from his face with his shirt.

"He's my son."

"For heaven's sake!" Qing Yuan said. The sun was relentless. The broiling sand was scalding his knees.

"Don't you remember?" the lab director said, almost whispering. "He denounced me at the struggle session yesterday. Lies and lies and nothing but lies!"

"The Red Guards were beating me, and I passed out."

"I'm sorry." The lab director paused for a moment. "My son," he said, and nodded to the captain, "that revolting little snitch, took a letter from my brother in Taiwan and gave it to the authorities." He rubbed his eyes with the back of his hand. "Now the State believes I'm a Kuomintang spy."

"Are you sure it was him?"

"He admitted it, proudly, in front of my colleagues at the office!" the lab director said, powerless to control his tears. "I tremble for my wife should she ever find out."

The broadcaster's voice droned on. The sun beat down. Qing Yuan's sweat poured from his face, yet his mouth was so dry he couldn't spit on the captain had he had the chance.

"You can't do this, you can't do this," the gynecologist groaned as she crawled about.

Two of the Red Guards, a boy and a girl, leapt into the pit. When they snatched the gynecologist, she let out a terrible scream and smashed her head into the girl's jaw.

The girl seemed unphased, as though she'd had her jaw smashed every day. She looked to Qing Yuan like someone reading a magazine. With a fistful of the gynecologist's hair, the boy flung back her head. Then, as if all this had been choreographed, the girl punched the gynecologist hard on the nose. Her glasses shattered. The blood shot out. The boy began to pummel her.

"I'm not a criminal!" the gynecologist screamed as the boy and girl dragged her by the hair up the side of the pit. "You can't do this!" The threesome disappeared, but the screams went on. "I'm not a criminal. You can't do this! I'm not a criminal!"

Qing Yuan wanted to collapse but willed himself to remain upright. Before him on the burning sand lay the gynecologist's destroyed glasses.

16.

They were shoved back into the darkness while the broadcast droned on. The mosquitos wasted no time resuming their assault. From time to time the lab director groaned beside him. Qing Yuan rested his head on his knees and wondered how many days had passed since he'd eaten with Lao Jia.

In all likelihood he had been cast into a darkness of his own. Their years of hardship and desolation had vanished. The days were long, he thought, but the years were short. The one merit he'd attained lay in his deep understanding of the anguish of mortality. Together he and Lao Jia had surrendered to the monotony of their life in the morgue. Ever hopeful in his cynical way, Lao Jia once said, "Fear might also be hope." But here in this darkness, amid the hissing of mosquitoes and the stench of sweat and coal and waste, Qing Yuan's hope was seeping away.

The sound of shoes clattered from the ceiling. An accordion played a revolutionary song. Some girls shouted, and others clapped. The song and the shouting grew louder with each verse. Soon the walls were shaking. He gazed blindly into darkness. His father, disfigured and frail, trudged in the distance, shackled with chains. He stopped and pointed to the sky. "The snow is falling, now, Son," he said, and trudged on.

The lab director was hauled off again. Qing Yuan strained to hear the conversations, the laughter, the invective. Then all fell away to silence. He wondered when it would be his turn.

"Mosquitos will fly twenty-two kilometers for a meal," the pediatrician whispered. "This is a proven fact."

"I've got enough blood to feed them all right here," Qing Yuan whispered.

This darkness, he thought. This was how they broke you. This was how a man lost himself. Dignity, virtue, kindness, love, the essence of his soul, even—everything was blotted out.

Images danced like clouds in the offing. His thoughts unraveled and melted away. Time and space had collapsed. He was a monad in the dark. Voices murmured through the ceiling, chair legs squeaked on the floor, boots and shoes stomped and slapped. An object struck the floor hard enough for Qing Yuan to fear the ceiling would collapse.

He began to count from one. And then the faces began to surge through his mind—#19's, destroyed, Feng Ge's husband's, dead and gray, Lao Jia's, resilient in its anguish, the captain's, the pediatrician's, the girl's, vicious and bright in the burning pit, the lab director's, the gynecologist's, terrified yet brimming with generosity and courage, the surgeon's, its arrogant pout.

His head was pounding. He realized he hadn't smoked since they'd taken him away. He'd been smoking packs a day for years. Hunger, for food and for nicotine, clawed through his guts and his veins. It was worse than the worst illness, he imagined, though he'd never really been ill. He spread his arms to ease the numbness that had beset them. His hand brushed the gynecologist's coat on the ground, and he smoothed it out and sat on it.

Abruptly, everything stopped—no motion, no sound, only eerie silence. Qing Yuan gripped his knees and waited for something, anything, to make itself known. He'd forgotten he wasn't alone. The pediatrician cleared his throat. He slapped himself two or three times. Then the noise through the ceiling struck up again.

"I lost a son," the pediatrician whispered, "during the Great Famine. My daughter always says that, being a doctor, I should have known better. Ever since, she and my second daughter have drawn pictures of their dead brother's eyes, hundreds, thousands, an endless pile of sketchpads filled with my dead son's eyes. 'He can still see us!' they say all the time. Old grief, new despair—it's a never-ending circle. It hasn't mattered how many times. Not once have I been prepared." He began to cough. "A sip of water sounds nice, doesn't it?" he whispered after the fit had passed. Qing Yuan slapped some mosquitos on his face but didn't speak. "The poor surgeon!" the pediatrician whimpered. "His destroyed hands, maimed now for life!"

A giant hammer swung through Qing Yuan's mind. He heard the tear of flesh, a rending cry. Blood dripped like wine from the ceiling. A man sullied his pants. A woman's body lay streaked with waste. He had been buried alive in blistering sand.

The gynecologist's coat had stuck to his back. It both horrified and eased him. The noise through the ceiling thundered on, and soon they heard footfall in the corridor, the clatter of chains and the bark of commands, nearer and nearer until whoever it was continued down the hall. A man began to rant. An engine revved. Tires peeled through gravel. The sound of the truck grew thin. Again there was only silence.

"I'm convinced," the pediatrician hissed as he slapped himself, "that I've had more mosquito bites than the rest of you together. But then that's always been the case. My daughters call me the 'mosquito-magnet.'"

Quin Yuan's qi had disintegrated into nothing. He had nothing with which to move, not even his mouth, nothing to say if he could. The pediatrician asked whether he had any children.

"I'm not married," Qing Yuan whispered after a time, and thought of Feng Ge. He couldn't remember how many days had passed since they'd parted but could recall every moment with her. They had melded in the vision of a new life in which their suffering and pain would drain away with the years. They had dared to imagine stability and peace. Dreadful as their reality was—his nights in the morgue cleaning the dead, Feng Ge's grief, the poverty and the uncertainty—hope had sprung up between them like a flower through late spring snow. How she had blushed when he had mentioned the notion of a new child in their imminent family. How they had laughed at the possibility. Their joy had been fragile but real. Qing Yuan, after having wandered the plains of loneliness for a lifetime, had somehow found an oasis in the dark.

"It's good that they arrested me at the hospital," the pediatrician said, his voice softer now. "Nothing could be worse for a child than to see their father arrested."

"They must be worried about you."

"My wife knows I'm here, but she'll never tell them."

Without warning, the door banged open, the lab director was hurled into the room, and the door banged shut. Neither he nor the pediatrician had heard the sound of anyone approaching.

"What's going on up there?" Qing Yuan whispered.

"The surgeon was taken away in shackles," the lab director said.

"Quiet!" the pediatrician hissed. "If they hear you, we'll all be taken upstairs again."

"By whom?" Qing Yuan whispered.

"His head was bleeding badly," the lab director said. "That's all I know."

"But his hands were already broken!" the pediatrician whispered.

"They made me read the *Little Red Book* to Mao's portrait," the lab director said.

"All this time?"

"That pretty lieutenant is meaner than she looks. Her face alone could cover the world in ice. I paused once to clear my throat, and she whipped me. Then she asked why I wasn't smiling. 'The Chinese are the happiest in the world,' she said, and ordered me to smile at Chairman Mao." He started to cough, but soon he was laughing maniacally. "If I could kill that little fucker, I'd be the happiest man in the world," he said.

Soon the door was flung open again. This time the boyish Red Guards dragged Qing Yuan from the room. He stood for a moment, swaying in the blinding light. They shoved his back as they passed some Red Guards pasting *dazibao* on the walls. They climbed a stairway and entered a classroom. The desks and chairs had been pushed against the wall and stacked almost to the ceiling. In the center of the room hulked a desk behind which sat a girl frowning over a file. The room's four windows, three with broken panes, were open. The door had been removed. It lay on the floor beneath a rolled-up mattress.

On the blackboard, in colored chalks and enormous letters, read, "Long Live the Invincible Mao Zedong Thought!" The letters had been written around a melon-sized sun haloed by drops of water. Mao Zedong glared from above the board.

"Here he is," one of the boys said to the girl at the desk.

She waved imperiously. The boys retreated to the side of the room.

Qing Yuan knew this was the lieutenant the lab director had spoken of. She wore a white shirt with a red armband, and green military pants. Her face above the file before her had pinched and darkened, as if she were disgusted. Her seemingly inviolate sobriety was at complete odds with the beauty of her face. Qing Yuan knew without looking that she had bound her breasts the way all female revolutionaries did.

A tiny girl with braided hair appeared. "Lieutenant," she said. "The captain asked you to start on your own."

The lieutenant opened a bottle of ink and filled her pen. The tiny girl joined her peers, lounging in a clump near the stacks of chairs.

"I sure am craving an ice lolly," she said.

"I'll get us some after this," one of the boys said. He'd been cracking a folded belt.

"Get one for me, too," another boy said.

"You still owe me three cents," the first boy said.

"How many of my ciggies have you smoked today?"

"Fuck you," the first boy said, and cracked his belt.

"You shut up," the tiny girl said. "You know it's wrong to swear."

The boy cracked his belt in the girl's face, and everyone laughed.

The lieutenant silenced them with one cold glance. She slapped the file against the desk and glared at Qing Yuan. "What have you been doing these past few days?"

The voice was at shocking odds with the lovely face it had come from. She sounded like a girl imitating a witch.

The sores on Qing Yuan's buttocks had become infected. He wanted to press a hand against them, but knew he couldn't. He stood there dumbly, confounded by this severe girl. She'd asked nothing about his background or his identity. He couldn't grasp the intent of her question.

She glowered at him. "What, I said, have you been doing for the past few days?"

"Sitting in a coal room."

"That seems like a perfect place for one to contemplate their guilt." Her eyes bore into his. "Have you been contemplating your guilt?"

"I've been working in the morgue for the last sixteen years. That is all I have done."

"Your father stole from the State."

"What did he steal?"

The girl slammed a fist on the desk. "You know very well that gold is national property!" Qing Yuan said nothing. "Were you with him when he hid it?"

"I was not," Qing Yuan said, and realized the girl was reading from a paper in the file before her.

"Did he *tell* you that he'd hidden it?"

"Yes."

"Who else did he tell?"

"My mother, perhaps. I don't know."

"So your mother knew, too, but chose a cowardly death to escape her punishment."

Rage coursed through Qing Yuan. He hadn't felt an emotion this powerful for years. Everything about his mother was sacrosanct. Her death itself had been graceful, despite her immense grief, at once a reconciliation and communion. She had given all and escaped nothing. *You little beast*, he thought, struggling against the urge to throttle the lieutenant then and there. *You know nothing but derangement.*

"My mother was the gentlest woman I have ever known."

"The Party does not frolic with dialectics! Here we deal only with the truth!"

Qing Yuan did all he could to suppress the smile that would insinuate the absurdity of this girl's arrogance. "Did your father have many concubines?" she said.

"Impossible," Qing Yuan said, and looked into the eyes of the monster before him.

"*You*," she said, pointing at Qing Yuan, "are wasting my time! Confess!"

"I've told you everything."

"It's obvious the darkness did nothing to clear the filth from your head."

"I understand."

"Do you understand that we know you better than you know yourself?"

"I've denounced my father. I've given up everything. I have given the Party everything."

"You disappoint me, Comrade." The woman-child shook her head.

"I signed the letter, Lieutenant."

She waved her file—Qing Yuan's dossier—at him then slapped it on the floor. "This," she said, pointing, "is perfectly complete. It is the embodiment of truth!"

"I am not a liar."

"In his confession," the lieutenant said, "your family steward said your father must have hidden the rest of his gold somewhere else. The only person who could know where is you, the steward said."

"That man's confession is worthless!" Qing Yuan roared. Not once in his life had he spoken in rage. It was exhilarating. "He lied and sent a good man to his death. He destroyed my family! He destroyed everything!" The lieutenant glared at him with delight. "I am a morgue keeper," Qing Yuan said. "That is everything and all. I deal with the dead and only the dead."

The lieutenant snatched up her bottle of ink and flung it at Qing Yuan. It struck him squarely on the brow.

The teenagers, who the moment before had been bickering about ice lollies and cigarettes, swarmed on Qing Yuan as fast as he could fall. The first boy to reach him kicked his back. The boy with the belt lashed his face. He tried to stand, but the blows went on until he felt himself being dragged away and down the stairs. In a moment the world had grown blindingly intense, and he was hurled into the sandpit. The lieutenant skittered in after him and kicked his head.

"If darkness won't purge you of your idiocy," she said, radiant with power, "let's see what this sun will do."

The sun was an inferno. Qing Yuan lay beneath it, like a louse on the blazing sand, unable to move. There was nothing but sand and sun and pain. From a far distance, as across a desert, his mother's voice came to him. "Is it dawn yet?" she said. Qing Yuan wanted to speak but couldn't move his mouth. "Is it dawn yet?" his mother said again, and all went black.

17.

His face lay wedged against the side of the pit. A young voice was screaming at him. Then someone kicked his head again. He could sense the scalding sand beneath him and the blinding sun overhead, but he couldn't open his eyes. He could no longer feel any pain. All he could see behind his eyelids was a thin blanket of stars sparkling against an infinite black. Someone snapped a belt by his ears, but Qing Yuan didn't stir.

"He's still breathing," a voice said.

"Ha! Not dead yet, eh?" It was the lieutenant. "Get this piece of garbage back to where he belongs," she shouted. Then some bony hands dragged him from the pit and raised him up. His face burned as if it had been scalded with hot oil. He didn't know where he was until he'd been hurled into the coal room, and the door had slammed.

"Is someone here?" he croaked.

"We are," the pediatrician whispered. "And so are the mosquitoes."

Qing Yuan groped toward the pediatrician and collapsed.

"They didn't break you, I hope," the lab director said.

"I'm all right," Qing Yuan said. He took his shirt off and put it over his face to shield it from the mosquitos. He felt himself shiver, hot then cold. An insect crawled along his chest. It occurred to him that in another life he'd want to be an insect in the dark. Row on row of open mortuary cabinets appeared before him, each of them stacked with bodies. He struggled to recall the faces of each corpse. He wanted to remember them all from his first day in the morgue until now.

The thousands of nights had become a single night of dead bodies, creaking doors, unbearable stench, the filthy "Serve the People" sheets stacked on the floor. He had always loathed the look of the dead, but now they alone could bring him peace.

He found himself in a cemetery searching for his parents' graves, though he couldn't remember their names. There were no trees, no grass, just dead weeds and sunbaked dirt. The odor of the ashes of cremated bodies made him swoon. A circus wagon drawn by colossal horses zigzagged across what seemed an endless plain. In time the wagon drew nearer, the chime of its bell punctuated by the clip-clop of hooves. Its canvas top featured blossoms and lively birds. It was the design, Qing Yuan knew, of the silk rug in his childhood drawing room. His mother called out from inside the wagon. "Come, my dearest, come!" The wagon passed, and his mother peered smiling out of the back. He ran toward the wagon. One of the horses broke free and charged his way. To escape, he plunged into the horse's eye. He was enveloped in golden light. A silver river ran through a meadow of butterflies and blossoms. He chased a long-tailed bird low on a breeze until the bird rose up and sped toward a stand of glistening trees. Qing Yuan stood alone in the meadow. He had died in the eye of the horse.

The door clanged open, and the captain called out. Qing Yuan rose, his body heavy as a planet, and struggled into his shirt. In the doorway, as ever, he paused, blind in the sudden light. The captain slapped his face, and he limped off to the toilet. His vision improved with each step. The gynecologist appeared, her torn clothes stained with filth and blood. Her face had been ransacked. It was obvious that one of the lieutenant's child-beasts had bashed her forehead with a club or stick. Her lips were split open. He couldn't say for sure, but it looked like a few of her teeth were missing. Her hair had been randomly cropped, some long, some short. One of those little monsters had sheared it away with a dull knife, he thought. Her eyes wheeled like a maniac's. He passed her, his gaze to the floor, and saw blood oozing from her toes.

"Where is the rest of my wolfpack of intellectuals?" she shouted.

Qing Yuan glanced at her but couldn't speak. The guard had been shoving and poking him all along.

After the toilet, Qing Yuan limped back to a tin on the floor and slid down the wall. The gynecologist, cackling, had been left to stalk the corridor, perhaps as a warning to the prisoners who refused to submit.

"You look like a clown," she said, "a stunning handsome clown!" She threw back her ruined head, cackling. "But then again, we're all of us stunning, yes?" She set her hands on her knees and swayed as if dizzy. A thin line of drool spun from her mouth. Her teeth, Qing Yuan saw, were indeed broken. She coughed and lurched toward the tin by Qing Yuan, but before reaching it, she slumped against the wall and began to hum a melody that sounded like an old-time lullaby.

Qing Yuan hadn't realized the others had also been let out. They raised their tins to their mouths and forced the pabulum down. The gynecologist squatted next to Qing Yuan. He couldn't imagine she'd have strength left to eat, the pain she'd endure putting food into her mouth. She picked the cornbread from the tin and slurped once or twice at the porridge. Then she flung it away and crawled to the pediatrician on the other side of Qing Yuan and dropped the bread in his porridge.

"*You* eat it," she said. The pediatrician grimaced. She snorted, then crawled back to the slop on the floor and licked it. "Too much salt but no water," she said. "No water, no water, no water."

A Red Guard appeared and slapped her face several times. "Bring me a mop!" he shouted to a boy down the way. "You fucking bitch," he said, and punched the gynecologist hard on her nose. Blood shot out, but the gynecologist didn't raise a hand.

"No water!" she screamed. "You give us no water! You give us no water at all!"

The other guard returned with the mop. The first guard boxed her ear. "Clean this shit, now," he said, "or you'll get worse than you've already got."

"No water!" she screamed. "No water! No water! No water!"

The second guard snatched her by her smock and thrust the mop at her. "Do it now," he said.

To Qing Yuan's surprise, the gynecologist began to swab the floor. "I've starved before," she sang as she went. "1959, 1960, 1961! Three years of starvation! I'm not afraid of hunger," she said. "It's you who should be afraid!" she said, and pointed at the guard who'd struck her, now down the hall. She turned to Qing Yuan and snapped. "Are you afraid of starving? Because you will! All of you will starve!"

"Please," Qing Yuan whispered. "Please take it easy."

She threw back her head again. "I have my period," she crowed, "but they give me no pad, not even a bit of paper! Nothing!" she screamed, "nothing but *salt*!" Tears streamed down her ruined face.

"Shut the hell up!" the guard yelled from the end of the hall. "Do you actually want some more?"

She crammed a hand down her pants and yanked out a shred of blood-soaked yellow paper. "Ha ha ha ha!" she howled. "Here's your *dazibao*! It's all blood, now. Here, and here, and here!"

The two guards rushed back shouting and wrenched her arms behind her. They were just boys, Qing Yuan saw, angry brainwashed teenagers. They heaved the gynecologist to the floor and began to slam her head into it. They didn't stop until she lay motionless in their hands.

"If any of you want to join her," the second guard said, "this is what you'll get."

By now the captain had appeared. "Get that piece of shit out of here!"

To everyone's astonishment the gynecologist cocked her head and screamed. The two boys dragged her off, yet still she went on. "The five of us, let me return, my wolfpack! I'll sing for you. *The east is red, the sun is rising. From China comes Mao Zedong!*"

The guards ignored her. This was not the first time they'd reduced a human to a slimy beast. Her voice grew hoarser. By the time they'd turned the corner at the end of the hall, she had no voice left.

"I have a plan," the lab director whispered. He licked his fingers and grimaced. "I'm going to kill him. The captain."

"He's your son!" Qing Yuan hissed.

"What I'll do in no way represents a father killing his son. It will be a man killing a creature who is a disgrace to the name of man. They can send me to the firing squad afterward. I will have done what needs to be done."

"Do you have any idea how crazy that is? Have you thought of your wife?"

"I'm a scientist. My job is to analyze human specimens, recognize anomalies, and interpret them. With a microscope, I'm able to see cells no one could with the naked eye and know when a good cell has gone rogue. If not killed quickly, cancer is born. That fiend," the lab director said, nodding toward the end of the hall, "is a rogue cell, an evil to society. This is a sooner-the-better case. I was one of the two who brought him into the world. It's my job to escort him from it. The rats in my lab are killed all the time."

Qing Yuan could say nothing to this man who had made up his jangled mind. He put his face in his hands.

The two guards and the captain had returned and were smoking at the end of the hall. The pediatrician set down his tin and rose. "I might as well go again while I can," he said. He smiled with great peace at the lab director and Qing Yuan then moved off with his head held high.

The two sat in silence. The pediatrician didn't return. Ten minutes passed, at least.

"What's happened to him?" the lab director whispered.

"What's happened to him?"

"Can he really still be in the toilet?"

Qing Yuan looked at the pediatrician's tin on the floor, its cornbread still floating atop the untouched porridge, and felt like he'd been punched.

"Something's wrong!" he shouted, and scrambled to his feet. "A man is in the toilet. He hasn't come back!"

"Just shut up and eat," the captain said, then ordered one of the guards to investigate.

The guard opened the door to the toilet and stood there gawking. "Come quickly!" he said.

The pediatrician had cut his throat with a shard of glass from the broken window.

18.

Qing Yuan lay sick on the coal. Ulcers had gnawed into his buttocks and hips. The rest of him throbbed with blisters and bites from the mosquitoes and the vermin. His knees had been scorched by the sand, and now in the hot damp of the room, they, too, were infected. He was sick, and sickened by his sickness. He was decaying, he thought, as surely as the bodies in his morgue.

He'd never considered, not even jokingly, not even drunk, that he would miss that place, and yet here he was in this blasted dark, wishing he were there, ready after a long night to meet with his friend Lao Jia. How absurd was it, he thought, to have grown dependent on a solitude he could find only with the dead?

"The moment they let me out of here," he remembered the pediatrician saying, "I'm going to hit the nearest grocery, buy a half kilo of baijiu, and glug it all down on the spot!"

Lao Jia would have slapped the doctor on his back had he been there to do it. Qing Yuan remembered very well the baijiu Lao Jia had shared with him his first night in the morgue. The last time he had drunk with Lao Jia was the evening he told him about Feng Ge. The two days could have been many or one. The endless dark had stripped him of time. He subsisted in a void absent days and nights. He could feel and taste and touch and hear, but he couldn't see, nor, he found, trying in vain, could he move. He couldn't say his memories were true. He couldn't say he had a mind with which to remember. He *thought* this or that may have happened only to doubt himself the next moment. Lao Jia's anguished face hovered before him. His voice, not from his mouth but from the darkness in which Lao Jia's head floated, whispered at Qing Yuan the story of his days, his wife raped, his boys murdered, his wife dragged dead from a river after Lao Jia had abandoned her. Feng Ge had wanted to meet Lao Jia, she'd told Qing Yuan more than once.

"It's incredible," she had said, he remembered, "that your bond has held for sixteen years. Your friendship has survived when so much else has not."

Now and then his meanderings were spoiled by the lab director. Here, the man would groan. There, his voice like an ice pick would blasphemy the dark. "You fucking little bastard parasites!" he'd shout as he slapped himself. "I'll kill you and all your stinking kind! I'll kill you," he'd shriek, slapping and slapping, "and you, and you, and you—I'll kill you all!"

Qing Yuan knew the lab director was lost when at one point— Qing Yuan couldn't say when, he no longer knew the first thing about where-this or when-that—the lab director began to mumble like a man in a nightmare. "I'm running and running . . . It's a marathon, this . . . I'm only a messenger, but victory is ours . . . Or it would be a victory," he said, and clapped, "if I could kill you!" He went on mumbling and clapping. "I'm a messenger, a marathon messenger, here to report victory . . . I'll kill you all, I will. I will kill you all!"

Dizziness took Qing Yuan any time he opened his eyes. He knew a place full of life existed beyond the darkness, a place where his senses would be the compass by which to find his way. To see and feel and touch and smell and taste, to think and to know, these were the things from which kindness and love and compassion sprang, and sometimes hatred, and sometimes rage. His world there in the darkness had become a vortex of absurdity and nonsense. In this timeless space he'd seen his parents emerge from the black in a circus wagon. Now they were there, again, holding hands beside a river in a meadow in full bloom, circled by trees that sang. They were happy, his mother and father. He soared with joy to see them as he'd known them. He longed for those days again. They'd never come, he knew.

And then they vanished, and the morgue appeared. He opened the cabinets one by one to whisper a prayer for each of the dead. None of them answered. He prayed even so. He would have loved them in life had he been there to love them.

Once, in his delirium, he stood by as a great flood engulfed the city. People, like untold millions of ants, stumbled and shrieked, desperate for their lives. The water rose to his chest as he stood alone on the street. All around floated garbage and filth. A baby's red shoe embroidered with a tiger's head swirled into his chest. The tiger squinted at him like he was prey. "Can you see *the smack of doom* on my face?" he said to the tiger. "Tell me the truth, please, before I die." The tiger said nothing. A baby wailed somewhere nearby. He cast about. The people had escaped. Enormous birds glided overhead. They crooned like the pigeons of his childhood as they perched on the boughs of the persimmon trees.

A figure in white waved at him then faded into the void. Feng Ge spoke in his ear. "I've carried a man's death. Now I smell another." He asked himself where the darkness began and would it somehow end. "Death is not a curse," Feng Ge said. "The darkness is the curse." Her voice became his father's. "Have you forgiven me?" he said. "You selfish bastard!" Qing Yuan said, disgusted with himself. He'd never used such words with his father or spoken to him in a such a tone. Yet he went on. "You'll never know how it feels in the morgue! You and your damned gold bars!"

The door flung open. A Red Guard ordered him out. Qing Yuan dressed as quickly as he could.

The lab director cried out. "You can't leave me here alone!"

"I'll come back," Qing Yuan said.

"You'd better!" the lab director shrieked.

Qing Yuan trudged down the hall, blind in the light. A girl shot out of a door and scurried away. Flies circled the door to the toilet. The door had been padlocked. The stench of death was incontrovertible. Qing Yuan understood. They had left the pediatrician dead where he lay.

The guard bullied Qing Yuan past this door and that until he was shoved into a tiny room, windowless and empty with but a small bare bulb flickering on the wall.

"Aren't you the lucky one!" the lieutenant said. This startled Qing Yuan. He hadn't seen her, though she was but two or three feet off, sitting on a student desk, swinging her feet like a child. "The hospital wants you back." Her lovely face could have been a sculpture of rocky ice crafted by a master. "You must report to your manager every day. You must attend all struggle sessions in the hospital and at Worker Village." He wanted to look away but couldn't. Her face was pearlescent and fanatical. "Never forget, ever—you are under the surveillance of our revolutionary masses," she said. She pointed to the door. "Now get out of here."

19.

He limped into the sun shielding his face with both hands. The lab director lay in the coal room alone. Qing Yuan could not go back had he wanted to. He should not have promised to return.

A bus pulled up. Two older men and several women jostled as they boarded. He couldn't join them. The Red Guards had stolen his money. Women with baskets glowered at him. He stumbled on, down a cinder path behind a dilapidated tenement. Three little girls stopped before him and plugged their noses.

"He smells like dead fish!" one girl said.

"He looks like a ghost!"

"A dead ghost!"

It took him an hour to reach Worker Village. At the path to the entrance, he saw Fan Fan in the shade of the willow outside the coal shop, picking nits from her hair. A colony of flies swarmed about her ragbag and tin. News blared from one of the ubiquitous speakers. He looked away, hoping she wouldn't see him, but she already had. She popped up with surprising agility and shouted.

"Sir! I've been worried! I haven't seen you for weeks." Qing Yuan knew he couldn't escape. "What happened to your face?" she said. "And your leg?"

"Where did you get that?" he said, and gestured to the badge of Mao Zedong's face on her chest.

She beamed. "Pretty, isn't it? A Red Guard girl gave it to me at the parade a few days ago." She fondled the badge with her blackened fingers. "I've never owned a piece of jewelry."

"So you joined the Revolution, did you?"

"If they accepted me, I would. It would be even better if they fed me!" Qing Yuan wanted to smile but couldn't. His desire for sleep was consuming. "But you," she said, "I've been so worried. Where have you been?"

Qing Yuan had already moved on. He passed into Worker Village. Most of his neighbors stared. The rest darted into their homes.

His doorknob had been bound with rusted wire, the doorway itself sealed with official paper. He ripped it away and untangled the wire.

The contents of his bureau and cabinet lay helter-skelter about the room, and his dishes had been smashed. The pillows had been ripped open, their buckwheat fillings everywhere. The windows had been smashed, as well. People had defecated on the floor, the counters, the table, his chairs. His wash basin was brimful with stinking urine. Flies swarmed everywhere. On the wall, in purple chalk, some ignorant neighbor had scrawled, "drink are pee you fucking basterd."

Like people at a crime scene, his neighbors gawked at him from his window. He ignored them and collapsed on his bed and descended into instant sleep.

He woke to morning sunlight, the door and window still open. He lay there a while, trying to find himself. Nearby, a neighbor's door creaked, and farther off an old woman coughed. He was ravenous with hunger. His whole body ached. He got up and tiptoed around the glass on the floor. His tote dangled from a peg on the wall. He rummaged through a mound of rags and salvaged a shirt and pair of soiled pants. He clawed his sneakers from under the bed then stuffed them and the clothes into the tote. His fruit knife and clock had been knocked to the floor with everything else. The clock was still ticking, though its face had been destroyed.

With the knife he unscrewed the back cover to get at the small roll of bills and ration stamps he had secreted there.

At a breakfast stand sided with tin he joined the middling queue. A number of people turned to him with wrinkled noses and scowled. He slavered at the sight of youtiao and shaobing. The woman behind the window eyed him with disgust.

He squatted behind the shack and devoured the food, swallowing more than chewing. He returned to the window and bought more shaobing, plus a bowl of wonton soup. The woman ladled it from a giant aluminum pot into a bowl lined with cracks. She drizzled vinegar into the soup and sprinkled white pepper over the top. Back at his spot he shredded the shaobing into pieces and dunked them in the soup. It was piping hot, but he chugged it down like water from a spring.

He bought cigarettes at a bodega and lit one the moment the clerk handed him the pack. He smoked it down then lit another and hobbled to a nearby bathhouse.

It was quiet inside. He was mesmerized by the steam, dizzy as he dragged himself to the changing room. A man collected his ticket and handed him a basket. He stripped off his clothes and shoes and stuffed them in the basket and slid into the water. He slumped against the side of the pool and fingered the bruises on his face.

He left the bathhouse and wandered down a street whose shops, though open, were mostly empty. A man was pasting a poster on the wall. A plump woman stood at the ladder, one hand on it and the man's ankle in the other. Another man slouched in the doorway, smoking as he watched. Once the man had stepped away from the ladder, the other man hopped into the road to squint at the poster. It featured a quote from Mao Zedong. "Our mission," it said, "is to make the enemy passive."

"It's fucking crooked," the man said.

The first man rubbed the glue from his hands and shrugged.

Qing Yuan smoked two more cigarettes before entering an

eatery down the street. The room was long and narrow with tables of raw wood at which a few men sat hunched over their bowls. The bath had inflamed the festers on his buttocks. They burned when he sat down.

Feng Ge and Sister Zhou were kneading dough on a table behind the counter. Sister Zhou moved off to feed the dough through a noodle maker. Her eyes met Qing Yuan's when she turned. She looked away and hurried to whisper into Feng Ge's ear. She froze. Then she wiped her hands on her apron and disappeared through a back door, Sister Zhou close behind.

A tall woman approached him. "You can't sit here," she said. Most of the diners turned to stare at Qing Yuan. "I know who you are. If you've come to see anyone, I can tell you now, they don't want to see you. Actually, it's not even possible to eat here." She poked a finger dusty with flour at a banner on the wall. "See that? '*Proletarian* Canteen.' That means there's no place here for counterrevolutionaries." Qing Yuan glared at the woman and clenched his jaw. The woman didn't budge. She stabbed an arm toward the door. "Now, fuck off!"

He went into a grocery store. Its windows had been shuttered with planks thick with *dazibao*. The stench of rotten vegetables permeated everything. But for the three women jabbering in chairs behind the counter, the place was empty. The moment they saw Qing Yuan, they fell silent and eyed him with open suspicion. After a time one of them came to serve him.

"One bowl," he said.

"Only one?" the woman said as she studied him up and down.

With the tail of his shirt Qing Yuan wiped the dust from the bowl then set it back down. "Baijiu, please."

"How much?" the woman said.

"Fill it."

The woman filled the bowl with a ladle. "Twenty cents," she said, as if speaking to someone Qing Yuan couldn't see.

He laid a fifty-cent bill on the counter. The moment she

placed the bowl before him, he snatched it up and drained the baijiu without pause, then returned the bowl to the counter and asked for more. He downed it like he had the first and left without his change.

On the street he stood gazing into the empty bowl. A sunbeam had inflamed its bottom. It seemed tremulous, almost alive. He could have been cradling an orb of fire. The pediatrician's face emerged from the flames then faded away. Qing Yuan smashed the bowl on the street.

20.

He lay in bed for two days, rising only to relieve himself, to make tea, to nibble the fried wonton strips he'd bought on his way home, and to empty his ashtray. He wanted to lie there forever but knew he'd already taken more time to return to the morgue than he should have. It wouldn't have surprised him to find men waiting to take him again. Should that happen, he knew, it would be the end.

Dazibao had been pasted on the walls, layer over layer, inside and outside the morgue. Lao Jia's name glared from many of them. The ground was strewn with cigarette butts, crumpled paper, loose *dazibao*, bits of food, spittle, mud.

Inside, Qing Yuan found the new man, Kong Jiu, mopping. A mound of bloody sheets lay in a corner. Qing Yuan tapped on the door and told Kong Jiu he was back. Kong Jiu seemed dismayed but did his best not to show it. He stabbed the mop into its pail and dragged it to the toilet.

Qing Yuan sat at the desk in the workstation rearranging the piles of forms, the stapler, pen, and bottle of ink. Kong Jiu walked in and stripped down to his briefs to wipe his body with a towel. Qing Yuan asked what he knew about Lao Jia. He was dead, Kong Jiu told him. They had sentenced him at a struggle session in the hospital. That was all he knew. He told Qing Yuan that if he wanted more information he should ask Qi Chu.

"He was there," Kong Jiu said. He had finished dressing. Qing Yuan watched, numb, as Kong Jiu gathered his things and left.

"How many?" Qing Yuan said.

"Nineteen," Kong Jiu said without turning.

That number again! What did a man have to do to find some modicum of grace? He had been tortured for well over a month. He'd returned to the morgue to be told that Lao Jia was dead and, in the same breath, to be assaulted once again by the ghost of a slaughtered woman he had promised satisfaction one way or another.

He knew how Lao Jia had been killed. He'd been executed. Why he'd been executed, however, posed yet another absurdity. Lao Jia, from what Qing Yuan could tell across their long friendship, had done nothing to give the State reason to believe he was a counterrevolutionary, unless of course Lao Jia or some distant relative had committed a so-called crime that he had kept secret. Yet the State didn't need a "reason." The "reason" was no more than a beard. Once a so-called fact had been engraved in a person's dossier, if the State deemed that fact treacherous, the person the State had accused would sooner or later be found guilty and punished as the State deemed fit. But Qing Yuan didn't care about these matters, now. His best friend was dead. This was the *fact*.

And no sooner had Qing Yuan learned this fact than it was married to the death of an anonymous woman slaughtered beyond recognition for reasons no sane person could justify. There was no reason for anything anymore.

Qing Yuan could not accept any of this. Yet nothing he did would bring back either of these murdered people. He knew the so-called reason Lao Jia had been killed. #19, on the other hand, in the larger sense, had been innocent. The very least he could do was to learn the circumstances of her murder. It didn't matter that her murderers were captured and punished. The likelihood of that, he knew, amounted to the escape of a rhinoceros from a zoo. One way or another, he had to find out. The incomprehensibility of a heap of bloody flesh and bones dropped from the sky before him haunted him no less than did the murder of his father and, in the wake of that, the quick death of his mother. He would find out.

Five gurneys lumpy with bloody sheets waited in the corridor. Kong Jiu wasn't the neatest man, this much was obvious. Qing Yuan felt both saddened and amused to see how fast the man had been anesthetized to his new "life" in the morgue.

It seemed for a moment that the entire world was a swirling amorphous ghost. The sight of the gurneys swooped him up and tossed him back to his first day at the morgue.

He had walked in to find Lao Jia humming "The Internationale" just as he was drawing one of five gurneys—*five*, Qing Yuan thought, five exactly—into the morgue. And on each of the gurneys lay the corpse of a construction worker who'd been killed when his scaffolding had collapsed.

Qing Yuan had had no idea what to expect before he'd arrived that long-ago first day. He knew that he'd be cleaning corpses, that was what he'd been told, and had donned a smock, a cap, and a mask, believing they'd act as a barrier between him and the bodies with which, against the whole of his will, he'd soon be forced into ghoulish intimacy.

"Get me a bowl of water," Lao Jia said to Qing Yuan, as if he'd known him for years. Lao Jia wiped the dirt and blood off the dead man's face. "Come here and watch. You get to clean the next one," he said, and flicked his cigarette into a corner. "They're not paying me to train you. I told the director I'd do this for three days. That's all you need. It doesn't take a college degree to clean dead people." He dabbed the face with his rag and flapped a cloth duster over the body. Finished, he commanded Qing Yuan to help him turn the body over so he could dust its backside, as well. Then they turned it right-side up and amended its posture.

From a cabinet in the corner Lao Jia selected five caps. "It's a circus here," he said. "We have all kinds of costumes and props." He placed a cap on the body's head. He pulled the brim low to cover as much of the face as possible. Qing Yuan could see that Lao Jia had done this many times. "These caps work a treat. They look cute on women, too," he said, winking at Qing Yuan. "Another thing. Don't forget to remove them before the bodies are sent to the crematorium. We need them for the circus!" He stepped back to survey his work. "Listen, little brother," he said, "we're not morticians but *morgue keepers*. We do our best, knowing in the end they'll never look right." He covered the body with a sheet stenciled with one of Mao Zedong's favorite mottos, "Serve the People." He slid the corpse into a cabinet then handed Qing Yuan his filthy rag. "Your turn, now," he said, and wheeled the empty gurney back to the corridor.

He returned with the second corpse then stooped down with a mock grimace to study its broken face. He brushed away a strand of sticky hair and tidied the collar. He nodded to Qing Yuan to begin.

Already the water in the bowl had turned gray. "Shall I change the water?" Qing Yuan said. His mask had done little to repel the noxious stench. He felt he might vomit, but shame obliterated the nausea. He could not degrade himself on his first day, before this strange new man.

"What for?" Lao Jia said, and resumed his awful song. Qing Yuan mopped his brow with a sleeve and dipped the rag in the bowl but couldn't bring himself to touch the corpse's face. "You'll feel better if you take that fucking muzzle off," Lao Jia said. He paused a moment. "I bet you're the kind," he said, "who reads stuff like 'Strange Tales From a Chinese Studio.' You believe in ghosts, I bet, fox spirits, immortals, demons—all that shitty paranormal stupidity." He drew his flask from his pocket and swigged from it, then smacked his lips and let out a sigh of deep satisfaction.

Qing Yuan had never met a man like him. His world, he thought, had become the caricature of some brutal theater. Lao Jia cocked his head. He looked like a tickled sage.

"But take it from me, kid, there are no ghosts. These lads here are still humans, and they are at peace. It's we who suffer, and who'll go on suffering till our own times come. Now," he said, leaning into the corpse, "look at this face." When Qing Yuan did no more than glance down with obvious reluctance, Lao Jia said, "Closer! Really look!" The corpse's face wasn't a face so much as a skull with battered flesh and hair. "Okay," Lao Jia said. "It's rough, I know, but the sooner you get used to it the better off you'll be." Lao Jia drew away the corpse's sheet. "Clean the face as best you can then give his clothes a good going over. And don't take your time. There are three others out there and more to come. The shift has just begun."

Qing Yuan removed his mask. He dabbed the face with his nasty rag then flapped the duster over the body. Lao Jia stood by watching. When Qing Yuan had finished, they performed the ritual they had with the body before.

"That damned director," Lao Jia said, "did a big favor to the construction company, getting us to clean these bodies. They have to cover their asses before notifying the parents. The company knows those parents and brothers would show their teeth if they saw their kids like this! If only you knew what these monsters do. It's all about the deadlines. They made these lads work the night shift by moonlight without a single safeguard in place! Just last week, three other boys younger than these fell off their scaffolding and died."

Qing Yuan couldn't fathom growing inured to sharing his air with the dead. He fixed his gaze on a sign on the wall. "No Smoking. No Spitting," it said. In short order they had tended to all five bodies. Lao Jia wiped his hands on his smock and lit a cigarette.

"There it is," he said. "What do you think?" Qing Yuan pinched his lips and said nothing. "By the way, it's our job to clean the floor at the end of the shift. I'll show you later."

After three days of training, Qing Yuan had to face the night alone. As they crossed shifts, Lao Jia said, "Little brother, don't forget to wipe your snot away when you burst into tears! If a ghost starts beating you up, fight back. No one else will be here to save you! And another thing. If you hear a voice coming from one of the cabinets, answer! They get lonesome in there sometimes and fancy a chat. Oh, and always keep your fly buttoned. It may surprise you, but they can be greedy. But cheer up. You'll get used to it soon enough!" He took his baijiu from the cabinet. "This shit always helps," he said, and clapped a hand on Qing Yuan's shoulder. He slipped into his overcoat and was gone.

After tidying up the mess Kong Jiu had neglected, Qing Yuan swept the corridor from end to end. He ached head to foot, but pushed on, chuckling a bit at the thought of Lao Jia's musical incompetence. He never could keep time. Now he was entertaining the cosmos with his slapdash song.

Qi Chu was late again, as usual, this time by an hour. "You're back," he said. A few minutes passed in silence. Qi Chu was studying him. "You're nothing but skin and bones."

"Is it true Lao Jia's dead?"

"They announced it in a struggle session."

"Did you see it, his execution?"

"He'd already been killed. We were only there to hear the reason."

"*We?*"

"Everyone in the hospital," Qi Chu said.

"How about his ashes?" Qing Yuan said.

Qi Chu scowled. "Lao Jia doesn't have a family. You know that."

Qing Yuan had never found out where the State had disposed of his father's body, and when his mother had been cremated, Gugu had refused to retrieve her remains. He couldn't look at Qi Chu. He took up his tote bag and left.

"Hey!" Qi Chu said. "How many?"

Like Kong Jiu had earlier, Qing Yuan did not look back. "Fifteen," he said.

21.

He bought a wash basin, bed sheets, a teapot and cups, a pail and some chopsticks, a big spoon and a knife, some glasses, some bowls, some plates, all with the hope that he'd seen the worst, that if he hadn't been forgiven, he might, with a bit of mercy and luck, be left to himself. He bought glass and caulking and putty, and a putty knife and box cutter and glass cutter and screwdriver and screws to replace the glass in the window and door. He installed a new lock. He scrubbed every nook. He bagged the trash and hauled it to the heap by the river.

A few days passed. Everything seemed more or less well. On the fourth day, he returned from the morgue to find the place worse than it was the day he'd been freed from the coal room. The windows had been shattered. Covering the table were piles of fresh stool. His basin was full of urine again, with new orders on the wall to "drink are pee."

He replaced what he could with the little money he had left but returned from work the next day to ruins, again—the feces on the table, the basin of urine, the moronic dictate above the basin scribbled by a new hand. He tried once more and returned the next day to more of the same.

He couldn't call the police. They themselves could have been the culprits. He stopped locking his door. One by one the few belongings that remained to him disappeared or were destroyed.

Most of his neighbors, some of whom he'd loaned money, slunk off glaring over their shoulders. Men he had bantered and smoked with veered into alleyways the moment he appeared. Once, a man whose life he'd saved, rushing him to the hospital after he'd fallen from his roof, slunk away without a word when Qing Yuan found him at the tap. Sister Zhou had shunned him, also.

The women ridiculed him. He was impotent, they said, he had nothing in his trousers but a mushroom. To the men he was a homosexual. "Rabbit," they called him, and "auntie." The youngsters were still more savage. "Hell ghost," they shouted as they threw bottles and rocks and anything else to humiliate or hurt him, rotten vegetables and paper bags full of stool. They called him "wild rabbit," and "foul-mouthed ghost," and "stinky egg," and "bourgeois ass-sucker," and "Soviet bastard," and "anti-Communist shitball." Boys and girls no older than seven or eight would trail him with their ruthless chants all the way to his door. Often it wasn't until one of his neighbors appeared to drive them away— not for his sake but because his assailants were disturbing *their* peace—that the children would relent.

Then he returned from the morgue to find a dead rat in his sheets and his pillow soaked with urine. He rolled up the bedding and dragged it away. He covered his bed board with newspaper and lay there naked, a small towel over his groin. The constant mob of rubberneckers made it impossible to sleep. He lay in a fugue state vexed by a parade of swirling corpses, the ruined faces of his youthful infatuations. Glistening dagger-toothed beasts leapt out from nothing. Old friends turned scoundrels abused him, the steward who'd betrayed his parents smirked with green teeth on a pile of gold. A dancing marionette-like Lao Jia croaked out the notes of a song Qing Yuan had never heard. #19 writhed on the table before him as her organs howled. The further he got from sleep, the more hallucinatory his visions became. The beautiful frozen lieutenant hadn't exaggerated one bit. Without doubt, he was under surveillance by the State and all its spellbound minions.

Dazibao appeared on his door and on the walls outside his room. To the last detail, his entire dossier had been published, most of it lies, of course. His life couldn't fit on a single sheet. This spawned more sheets, and those after them. Their sheer abundance, and the ugliness of their slander, not just of him but of his mother and father, too, all of it echoed by the community, saddened and enraged him. His father was now a notorious, unscrupulous, counterrevolutionary villain, a true smear on the good name of the Party. His mother had been branded a conspirator and bourgeois parasite. She had killed herself, the *dazibao* said, to escape her imminent punishment. Regardless of where he went, he knew, while he remained in China, his dossier would follow him as surely as his shadow.

One day he found a copy of the *People's Daily*, featuring a portrait of Mao Zedong. He cut out the picture and pasted it on his table. Anyone who wanted to shit here, he thought, would have to do it on the Great Leader's face.

The Revolution marched on with the brutality of the sun. The violence had become common enough to warrant no more mention for some than did a hole in their shoe.

Qing Yuan had been sweating naked through another of his visions, when two women and a man dragged him from the bed. He wrenched himself free and dressed as they stood by. They didn't wait for him to put on his shoes. The moment he'd buttoned his trousers, they marched him away.

A struggle session for the people of Worker Village had been scheduled to take place under the pagoda tree. Qing Yuan in his muddlement had forgotten it. A crowd had already massed in the courtyard. Row on row of wooden stools had been set out, all of them taken, yet the people continued to file in through the settling dusk. The air reeked of garbage, rot, burning coal, countless people rank without baths. Qing Yuan's escorts shoved him next to an old woman and a middle-aged couple. A burly man and a woman with a hair clipper stepped from the crowd. One by one the man wrenched their arms behind them as the chuckling woman shaved their heads.

She enjoyed her work. It was a game to her, Qing Yuan saw, as she rammed her clippers over the scalps of his fellows. By the time she had finished, each stood before the jeering crowd, their shorn heads rife with wounds and jagged bits of hair. Another man approached with paper dunce caps bearing the names of the accused and shoved them onto each of their bleeding heads. The man and the woman quietly wept. The old woman held fast with stoic resignation, refusing to be cowed. Qing Yuan was so numb he could do no more than watch with bleary-eyed detachment.

A cord had been wired through the branches of the tree from which dangled enormous blinding bulbs. A red banner hung festooned between two poles. "Once all struggle is grasped," the words proclaimed—yet another of Mao Zedong's abundant insights—"miracles are possible." A gang of teens, boys and girls, waved red flags.

Impatience swept through the crowd. Some of the women bickered. Others knitted or darned ragged clothes. The men kept together, smoking as they ogled the young women. Some shouted at their wives for dinner. Children skittered through the crowd like runaway thieves. Torture, Qing Yuan thought, had become a spectacle. Few if any had considered how far they'd had to stoop to embrace a joy born of savagery.

An old woman tottered through the crowd on her tiny bound feet. In one hand she held a stool and in the other a great palm fan.

"Grandma Bai," a man shouted, "how many days since it last rained?"

The woman plopped down on her stool and looked to the sky. "The dumbass doesn't even know how to count," she said loud enough for all to hear. "No need to look for your umbrella," she yelled to the man. "Your wife gave it to your best friend!" she said, and the people around her roared.

A cluster of little girls behind the old woman caught his attention. One of them, he realized, was Feng Ge's daughter, the girl he'd taken to the dermatologist to treat her afflicted hands. He saw when the girl clapped with her friends that one hand was still wrapped in a filthy bandage. His heart had ached for the child the instant he had seen her scrubbing laundry at the tap. That she might be his daughter soon, as Sister Zhou had encouraged him to hope, had filled him all the more with compassion. His head cleared. He smelled medicine and candy, he thought. He could smell Feng Ge herself, her ambrosial hair. His vision sharpened. His fatigue dropped away, and he felt no pain. Feng Ge had to be nearby. He couldn't speak with her, he knew, he'd never speak with her again. He wanted only to see her ample mouth one last time, her searching wounded eyes.

She'd been there all along with the children, impervious to the bedlam around her. One of the girls held up a handkerchief. Feng Ge took it and with her slender fingers folded the cloth into a mouse, then handed it to another girl, who passed it to her tittering friends.

Qing Yuan hoped she might gaze his way and smile. But she did not. She had not—would not, he knew—so much as glance his way. His heart had leapt at the possibility of seeing her. Finding her so remote shackled him again with weariness and pain. Loneliness gripped him. He couldn't recall such despair, not in the morgue, not in the coal room, not in the worst moments of his life. Bloody sweat burned his eyes. He struggled to muster his courage. This will pass, he told himself, his shame and fear would pass.

The old woman beside Qing Yuan began to quiver. Her wide-legged pants, made of brocaded silk, he saw, were split to her crotch, the handiwork of a Red Guard, exposing her inner thighs and underwear.

"The old bitch is shaking!" a woman jeered. "It won't be long till she wets herself, I bet!"

The mob roared. Qing Yuan reminded himself that this behavior wasn't innate in people. It had been loosed by force—the authorities goaded the people every day, all day, through the inescapable blaring speakers, appealing to the worst of their natures, threatening their livelihoods and their lives themselves—to track down and harass any so-called traitor in their midst.

The old woman's face had drained of color. She looked like a cursed figure in a classic painting. A scrawny woman rose with her knitting needles to tell the old woman she'd trade pants whenever she wanted. The mob roared like they had the moment before. The woman's husband waited for the applause to subside. "Sit down, you shameless cunt," he shouted, "or I'll kick your skinny ass in!" Once again, the mob cackled and jeered.

Another woman yelled that the old woman was worse than a whore. A man straightaway roared that the couple, both professors, were the most hypocritical enemies. The crowd's fury mounted.

Soon a scraggly fellow rose and motioned for the rest to quiet. He spoke like an actor on stage. "We proletarians worked hard to send our kids to school. These devils taught them nothing but hypocrisy and destroyed their futures. They paraded through Worker Village like we were their inferiors. We called them neighbors! But I ask you, did they ever return our goodwill? Our hands were too rough to shake, our words too coarse. Without a doubt they believed they were fated to rise above our misery and leave us behind forever. But because of this mighty Revolution, our eyes have been opened. I ask you, can we trust our children to them anymore?"

"No!" the people roared. "No!"

"No more intellectuals in Worker Village!" another man shouted. "Here or anywhere else! Down with these fuckers! Send them to the labor camp! Let them scrub our latrines and eat our shit!"

Qing Yuan struggled to stay on his feet. The faces before him, like those at the colossal struggle session before they had damned him to the coal room, contorted with hatred and rage, and with the stupidity that had birthed them. His chin fell to his chest. Through his fog, he knew he was drooling.

A woman with a baby on her hip rushed up to the couple and spat in their faces, back and forth until her mouth ran dry. While the mob jeered and roared, the couple stood motionless before them, the woman's spittle oozing down their faces. The baby started to cry.

"I did this for you!" the woman said to the baby. She made her way back to her stool. "I did this for my children," she cried. "I did this for my children, and for the children of my comrades!"

The youngest among the crowd began to circle the accused. They growled the names spelled out on the dunce caps. Like hardened fanatics, they hurled insults no child their age should have known. Two teenagers climbed the tree and pretended to urinate on Qing Yuan and his fellows. At the same time, the little ones pelted them with cinders and rocks. They struck Qing Yuan again and again. His numbness became his guardian.

Urine trickled down the old woman's legs. A puddle formed at her feet. Then she collapsed and began to sob. Applause exploded from the crowd. The woman who'd prophesied the old woman's collapse yelled triumphantly, "I told you! I told you!" Two Red Guards rushed over and struggled to haul the old woman up, but she clawed the dirt and buried her face in the mud her urine had made. For this, the Red Guards stomped on her back.

Several men jumped up, shouting about Qing Yuan.

"That morgue keeper is a class enemy, too!" one said.

"His father was a capitalist thief!" another said. "Banish him today, now!"

"Strip him down!" yet another said. "See what he's got!"

By now Qing Yuan was for all intents and purposes blind. A powerful kick struck his right knee and then another his left. As he staggered forward someone blasted his spine with what felt like a hammer. He crashed to the ground. His dunce cap tumbled to the feet of a teenaged boy, who stomped on it, then lurched forward to do the same to Qing Yuan's hand. He screamed. The crowd, ravenous, surged thundering in to rip away his clothes.

When he came to someone was hauling him to his feet. He

had been stripped to his underwear and pummeled and torn every inch. His entire body was thick with blood and dust and his wrists and knees were bound. At first he didn't register his tears. After a moment he realized with deep shame that he had been sobbing.

He woke in his bed in the dark, still naked but for his shredded underwear. His life hadn't abandoned him, he knew, though for a moment he wished it had. The outline of a figure backlit by pale light had been peering through the open window. Qing Yuan stumbled toward the switch near the door and saw the figure vanish.

In the jarring light he scraped some clothes from a drawer and a pair of sandals from under the bureau. The silhouettes of two men appeared in the doorway. "It's time to go to work," one of them said.

He was shoved into the bed of a three-wheeled truck. It wasn't long before they pulled up to the morgue. One of the men in the cab jerked a thumb at Qing Yuan and without a word he tottered toward the door.

Kong Jiu said nothing to Qing Yuan. He appreciated the silence. Kong Jiu seemed to intuit this. Eventually he gathered his things and left.

Qing Yuan had no idea how many corpses he had tended. He saw the clock reach 6 a.m. and lay on the table with his bottle. "A morgue," he remembered Lao Jia saying, "must be built on the ground. The dead enter the cosmos not through the firmament but from this very earth."

A willowy figure floated toward him. Sweet with a scent he'd never known, she lay an arm across his shoulders. He looked at her face. It was the gorgeous but brutal lieutenant.

"I'm just as scared as you are," she said, and he trusted her.

"My face has been cursed with the 'smack of doom.'"

"I see nothing," she said. She was caressing him. Her hands were cold.

"I have never disliked anyone."

"We're all going to die."

"It's not dark enough."

"I don't know." A knife appeared in her hand. "My blood isn't red like yours."

Qi Chu was bandaging his wrist when he opened his eyes. His clothes and the table were drenched with blood. Between his legs sat his empty bottle and a small paper knife. On a gurney a few feet off lay a fresh corpse covered by a sheet. Someone else had died in his place, he thought, though of course he couldn't be sure.

"Don't worry," Qi Chu said. "No one will know a thing."

22.

Throughout the city anything that moved raised clouds of yellowy dust. Women with straw baskets trudged along in their cloth shoes, licking their lips and coughing. The men stood beneath awnings and wilted trees sweating as they smoked. The heat had been foreordained. There would be no respite. On the corner of every block the so-called news blared from the omnipresent speakers.

He pushed along in the fumes behind a rickety bus, on his way to his aunt's for her birthday. A few blocks from her home, he stopped at the European Market to buy her a present. Years ago, this neighborhood had featured elegant townhouses and villas. Its streets had been handsome with shady *wutong* trees. At the heart of the district a garden had bloomed year-round. The place had bustled with posh locals and visitors alike, drinking, dining, shopping, reveling in the nightlife. The market was famed for its variety of gourmet delicacies. Many of the walks he'd shared with Gugu had ended at the market's café, where they splurged on ice cream or hot chocolate.

When the regime took over in 1949, the place was renamed the Red Flag Market. Paltry eateries, general stores, barber shops, weaving shops, grain stores, and daycare centers replaced the elegant bistros and boutiques. The marble statues at the garden's entrance were vandalized. The *wutong* trees were felled. Catawampus shacks appeared amidst the rubbish and weeds and even atop parts of the market building itself.

At the market's entrance, he was greeted by concrete and plywood thick with government notices and *dazibao*. The arched door and stone carvings that had once given him such delight had been demolished. The beautiful windows were covered with bricks.

A homeless couple squatted against a wall, the man picking his nose as the woman rattled a dented tin. Old women dug through piles of garbage. Two gray men were unloading crates of soy sauce and vinegar from the back of a rickety tricycle, while raggedy boys squabbled over cigarette butts and discarded bits of candy.

"Hello, sir!" Fan Fan said, when Qing Yuan returned for his bicycle with a boxed cake and two bottles of xifengjiu.

He wasn't surprised to see her, though he couldn't say he was glad, either. He hadn't wanted to see anyone, not even Gugu, if he was honest, despite that he had nothing but her, now, the sole remnant of his old life. It was her birthday. He had never missed it once.

"Where have you been this time?" Qing Yuan said.

Fan Fan poked her toe at an empty package of cigarettes. "I've always told you, sir, that a tramp goes where the wind blows." She fished out a few pieces of candy and handed one to Qing Yuan. "Feng Ge gave these to me after her wedding this morning. If you eat it, you'll have good luck."

He had welcomed his desolation. It had become an oasis of sorts, a refuge in a desert, its horizon in every direction—a thin fiery line empty of meaning or sense. Not to feel—to not have to feel, to be *unable* to feel, had without his knowing it at first amounted to a grace he couldn't until then have imagined. He had become insensible as a withered leaf. It startled him at first. Now he welcomed it, as it were, the way a stone might welcome rain.

He had known Feng Ge would find another, but hadn't guessed she would move on with such urgency. His love for her, not much more than a couple of months back, he reflected, struck him as having been a bittersweet illusion. The fates had been cruel to tease him so. Sister Zhou had essentially promised him a new life, and Feng Ge herself, with her graceful reception and sincere warmth, had been well on her way to fulfilling that promise.

The leap from numbness to aggrieved melancholy frightened him. He had believed, or perhaps only hoped, that his long misfortune had rendered him forever immune to such trifling horrors. For days he had eaten no more than scraps, yet now he felt he might vomit. The candy Fan Fan had given him weighed in his hand like a brick. He heard it clatter on the walk.

Fan Fan lurched down on all fours and scraped the candy into her mouth. "I'm sorry you don't like it, sir," she said.

She had been sheltering at the school on Victory Avenue. Victory Avenue, here or there on its long stretch, had been the site of #19's murder. Every time Fan Fan crossed his path, now, the image of #19's remains flashed to mind. He knew this would never change.

"Are you by chance still staying at that school?"

A shadow took her face, apprehensive but vulnerable. She poked at the empty cigarette package again. "It's an exciting time now, isn't it, sir?"

Qing Yuan handed her a twenty-cent bill. "It's my aunt's birthday," he said. "Buy yourself a drink."

At Gugu's, he considered how much her place, too, had changed. Until Mao Zedong had come to power, this big house had been hers alone. Then, within days of his father's execution, it had been appropriated, like every other piece of private property. What had been her living room was now all she had. The rest had been rented out, as Gugu had many times complained, to "an army of proletarians."

A rusty enamel bowl full of urine sat beside her door. Next to it was a dustpan and a large wooden bucket packed with coal.

He knocked, and straightaway Gugu opened the door. Her face turned white. "My boy!" she said, and began to sob. She took him in her arms, one hand on the back of his head. "My poor darling boy! What has happened to you?"

He passed by her, headed for the kitchenette. The place smelled of mildew, and of garbage and burning coal and the food Gugu was cooking. He set his packages next to a pile of plates covered with dish towels.

"Happy birthday!" he said.

"It means so much that you came, but look at you! Please, tell me, what has happened?"

"I lost some weight is all," he said, and conjured as peaceful an expression as he could. She gestured to a chair beside a mahjong table and poured him a cup of tea. She looked quite different herself, he thought, her brow and the skin around her eyes far more wrinkled than when he'd last seen her. She had cut her hair. Its severity emphasized her own desolation. "I'm not here to talk about myself. This is your day, Gugu."

"I don't care what day it is! I can see your bones! And your head! Surely you didn't do that yourself!"

Qing Yuan ran a hand across his scalp but remained silent.

She sipped her tea and pondered. "I was made to attend a struggle session," she said, her voice fraught with loathing. "They shaved Sister Wang's head and forced her to be a cleaner in a factory."

"Did they cut your hair, too?" he said.

"I knew it was coming, so I did it myself."

"It's lovely," he said. "You're as beautiful as ever."

"May I have a cigarette with you? Today is my birthday, after all." Qing Yuan gave her a cigarette and lit it. She pulled at it with obvious pleasure. "I don't keep them here," she said. "I'd start up again."

Everything the Party had left after they'd confiscated his family home had been sent to Gugu. She had stuffed the whole of it into her single room, right up to the ceiling. Over the years, as a matter of survival, she had had to sell most of it off, bit by bit.

His aunt had become two people. The first clung to the things of her past life—his mother's Ming wardrobe loomed from the wall like the shade of a crippled giant—as if fending off the solitude to which in the end she'd have to succumb. The second, temperamental, verging on collapse in the face of the cruelty around her, lingered paralyzed in the company of the phantoms with which she'd surrounded herself. She would never again find peace in this world, he knew.

She moved to the bed and stooped to retrieve something from under it. She turned to him holding a round basket lined with a ratty woolen shawl. "This is my surprise birthday gift," she said, on the verge of tears.

In the basket, with one tiny leg wrapped in gauze, lay a kitten.

"Where did you get this!" he said, and took the kitten.

A city ordinance forbade animals in any home. He and Gugu both knew that the creature's mere presence jeopardized them. It began to mewl when he stroked its head with a finger. The poor thing, striped with black and brown, no bigger than his hand, might as well have been in the coal room with him those endless starving days. It looked up at him, its eyes still blue, as if imploring him for something he didn't have. An unexpected warmth spread through him. He drew the kitten to his chin and hummed.

"I passed a rubbish heap this morning and saw her in a cluster of rags. The moment she saw me, she began to cry. She's no more than three weeks old, at best."

"But how will you feed her?"

"With soy milk, I suppose," she said. "It's all I have." He ran a finger along the kitten's mouth. It was nearly toothless. "I would take her to a vet if I could."

"Have you named her?"

"Xi'er."

"From that revolutionary play, *The White-Haired Girl*?"

"It has nothing to do with that play. It means 'happy girl.' And that's what she will be."

The kitten pushed its head into Qing Yuan's chest. He could feel its tiny pumping heart.

A muffled clamor reached them from the hallway. A door creaked open then slammed shut. Children scuttled about chirping and yelling. Smoke from a neighbor's stove seeped through the door. Qing Yuan's eyes began to water. Gugu stood up, switched on a light and opened the window. Already it had been too hot. Now a wave of heat rolled in. He could feel his brow dampening.

Gugu laid out matching plates and bowls and a set of chopsticks on each. Qing Yuan well remembered these, blue and white Chinaware featuring the painted story of two lovers turned into butterflies. His aunt had cherished the set all these years. She filled a pair of crystal glasses with the xifengjiu he had brought, then served up her meal. He returned the kitten to its basket at his feet and raised his glass.

"Please," Gugu said. "Let's not speak. I'm just so happy to see you."

They were about to drink when someone knocked at the door.

Gugu stiffened. She tiptoed to the door and pressed her ear against it. "Who is it?" she said.

Qing Yuan couldn't hear more than a muffled voice.

Gugu whispered over her shoulder. "It's Sister Wang!" Qing Yuan covered the kitten with the shawl, slid the basket under the bed, and returned to his seat. Gugu opened the door. "Please," she said, "come in. We were just about to have our dinner."

Sister Wang slipped in like a wraith, slender and bald and girdled with a pair of oversized horn-rimmed spectacles. "I'm so sorry to interrupt," she said, her voice both disturbing and melodic.

"It's no trouble at all," Gugu said, and took the woman's arm. "I insist that you join us."

"No, no," Sister Wang said. "Really, I can't. I was hoping you might spare a bit of firewood."

Gugu led her to the table and drew out a chair. She hurried to the kitchenette and returned with a plate and bowl, chopsticks, and another crystal glass.

"Your aunt told me you were still with us," Sister Wang said to Qing Yuan. "How glad I am to see you."

He lit another cigarette and observed the nun. She radiated with the aura of a woman remote in her wisdom and sorrow.

Gugu filled Sister Wang's glass and slid it toward her then raised a toast to both of them. "This isn't for my birthday," she said, "but for the good fortune that we can be together tonight."

They sat in silence, enjoying the sumptuous liquor.

"There's a struggle session this weekend," Gugu said. She gestured to the brick wall that had once been a French door. "She," Gugu said, referring to the neighbor who lived in what was once Gugu's dining room, a single mother with two sons and a disabled father, "told me last night." The woman, as Gugu said she often bragged, was a "communist cadre" in the Women's Federation.

Sister Wang shook her head. "She came to me asking for her fortune."

"But she just reprimanded you at the struggle session!" Gugu said.

"I told her," Sister Wang said. "'You can't believe what I believe.'"

"The communists are atheists," Qing Yuan said.

"She's desperate and afraid. She wants to know her future."

Qing Yuan toyed with his matchbox. He thought of #19, the awful stench of her. He thought of the superstition he'd lapsed into as he'd wandered the city searching for answers about her death.

"There was a woman," he said, looking Sister Wang in the eye, "a young one, I assumed, though really I couldn't tell her age. She'd been picked off the street and delivered to me." A spasm gripped his belly. He put his hands on the table and sighed.

Sister Wang bowed her head. In the growing dusk, her face seemed to emanate with soft light. Even her wrinkles, Qing Yuan thought, were captivating.

"You should have received another body that night," she said. "But you missed it."

"I received many bodies that night," Qing Yuan said. "It's a morgue." The room seemed to have devolved into a puzzling stillness. No one spoke. He'd been cast into another of his waking illusions. A truth struck him. It was as if a child had leapt onto his back. "She didn't die alone, did she?" he said, and tossed back the few drops left in his glass.

Sister Wang's eyes gleamed behind her ugly spectacles. She tapped a chopstick on the rim of her bowl. "You'll find out yourself," she said. "Your blood isn't what you think it is." She fastened her eyes on Qing Yuan's wrist. "I know you've seen it."

Despite the heat, he had worn a long sleeve shirt to cover his scar. No one but Qi Chu knew what he'd done. "What do you see?"

"It's as clear as water. Am I wrong?"

"It was dark."

"Everything is merely probabilities."

"Then how do you tell the future?"

"I look at your face. I can see it, but you can't, at least not in a mirror." She sipped from her glass and dabbed her lips with a handkerchief. "A mirror forgives human imperfections even as it fosters illusions. Once upon a time, the one way we humans could see who we are was in the depths of a sea or lake."

"That still doesn't tell me what I'm asking."

Qing Yuan looked at Gugu and realized she was worried the kitten might cry and give them away. She touched his knee under the table and raised her eyebrows.

"I say what I see," Sister Wang said, "though I seldom say all that I see. Too often most of us can't bear it." She traced the rim of her glass with a gnarled finger, round and round. "Myself included," she said, and tightened her lips.

An old man cursed in the neighboring room. A dish crashed against the wall. Then a faint cry emerged from under the bed. Qing Yuan and Gugu froze. Sister Wang's face remained inscrutable.

"Do you believe in reincarnation?" she said.

"I'm not a Buddhist."

Footsteps pounded above them. The thud of a laden bag or something else rather heavy followed. Qing Yuan slumped in his chair and stared at his hands face up on his lap. #19's body lay coiled in them, like a fetus. Flames engulfed her. Her fingers closed and dissolved into tiny paws. Fur, like velvety waves, sprouted along her arms and, with the flames, spread across her body. He looked into her eyes staring like a newborn child. The flames flickered and twisted. She leapt up graceful as a cheetah and flew away. A voice whispered in his ear. "I don't want the cosmos. I am here and will remain here. Never is never. Always is always. Everything is love."

He looked up at Sister Wang. She and Gugu were speaking in soft tones.

"My poor boy," Gugu said.

Sister Wang put a hand on Qing Yuan's wrist. "Take the kitten with you," she said.

23.

Kong Jiu sat dozing in the workstation. Qing Yuan set his duffle bag on the desk. Xi'er seemed to have grown used to the bag. It likely made her feel secure, Qing Yuan thought. But for the first few minutes he'd put her in the bag, on his way home from Gugu's, the kitten hadn't once complained.

When Qing Yuan brushed against Kong Jiu's arm, he lurched up and glared at him as though he were an assailant. "Don't ask how many, all right?" He ran his hand across his stubbly face. "There were so many—too many." Qing Yuan lay his hand on his colleague's shoulder and put a finger to his lips. "What's that?" Kong Jiu said, when Qing Yuan opened the bag and drew the kitten from it.

"A miracle."

"For heaven's sake," Kong Jiu said, like a boy before a gift. "Where did you get it?"

"My aunt. Her name is Xi'er."

Kong Jiu offered a finger to the kitten's nose. She sniffed it, then swiped at it with her tiny paw. "But how can she breathe in the bag?"

"I cut some holes on the side," Qing Yuan said. "She hasn't once made a sound."

"If someone finds out, you know they'll take her to the zoo for the predators to eat." Qing Yuan stared at the man, stupefied. He'd never considered such a thing. It seemed outlandish on the face of it. Who feeds kittens to beasts? "My neighbor works there. Any confiscated animal—dogs, cats, roosters, rabbits—is used as food for the lions and tigers. That's how they feed them." He saw his colleague's expression of horror and took the kitten and brought it to his chest. "I wouldn't bring her home," he said. "Your neighbors will turn you in, if they don't butcher her themselves."

Qing Yuan considered his broken windows, the urine-filled basin, the stool on his table each morning, the constant rubbernecking of anyone tall enough to peer into his window. It wasn't much safer at the hospital, though. He was under surveillance, that was certain. He spread the bag open in a corner and fluffed up Gugu's old shawl. Kong Jiu set the kitten on the little bed. It seemed to know this was home and rolled onto its back, swatting at Kong Jiu's fingers.

At his room Qing Yuan boarded up his window and covered the wood with pages from the *People's Daily*—photos of marching Red Guards, shouting crowds, fists raised high, Buddhist temples collapsing in flames. He installed a new lock on the door along with a padlock inside. He kept the lights off and moved like a thief. The times he wasn't sleeping he spent with the kitten. Several times a day, at the morgue and at home, he fed her with a spoon.

The once solemn workstation at the morgue transformed. Kong Jiu, who had been in an almost constant state of despair, began to stay after work to play with the kitten. He cleaned her litter box and refreshed the water in her bowl. He was so attentive, in fact, that now and then when Qing Yuan saw Xi'er bouncing around him, he found himself a little jealous.

Kong Jiu bought a pom-pom for the kitten. He tussled with her and scratched her almost incessantly. One moment Xi'er would yawn with lidded eyes, mellow under their hands. The next she'd pounce on them without warning, nibbling and biting them with her growing, needle-like teeth as she clawed their wrists with pumping back legs.

"Moody girl!" Kong Jiu would often say, pleased as a child. Each night when Kong Jiu gathered his things to leave, Xi'er would stand on her hind legs and paw mewling at his pants. "She likes me best, you know," Kong Jiu would say to Qing Yuan, and wink.

To his amazement, Qi Chu began to show up early for his shift. He cleaned a storage cabinet, drilled holes in its sides, installed a magnetic catch at the bottom of the door, and spread out a straw-filled mat he must have found on the street. The moment Qi Chu motioned that he was finished, Xi'er whipped inside and circled the space, sniffing about. When Qi Chu closed the door, she began to yowl. When he opened it, she sprang out and darted behind the stove.

"It's your home," Qi Chu had said. "Get used to it."

It wasn't long before she had adopted the cabinet as her own. Most of the time the door remained open for her to come and go as she pleased. The times it didn't were when people from the hospital came around on business, or when Qing Yuan had stepped away. Everyone knew the stakes. They put her in the cabinet at dangerous times. The door to the workstation was on the whole kept shut.

His time alone with her passed deceitfully. Whether minutes or hours had gone by, they seemed to him but a few breaths. Each time he was called away felt like being shaken from a gorgeous dream. He could think of nothing but her, and of being with her. Often she sat on his lap for hours as he sipped tea and plied her with stories from his childhood. Resting in the workstation, he pulled her to his chest and listened to her purr. If he dozed off, she would awaken him by playing with his nose or brushing her tail across his face. She watched him work with lackadaisical indifference but rushed up to paw him anytime she thought he might leave. The sight of her when he returned, purring as she circled against his legs, never failed to make him smile. He imagined her as sentimental. Her eyes, that blue melding now with an exquisite golden-brown, were to him unfathomable.

Then again, from time to time, she behaved like a petulant woman, he thought. She seemed angry and ignored him for reasons he couldn't understand. "What is it, little girl?" he'd say. "What did I do wrong?" She was just a kitten, he knew, but he had to confess his feelings had been hurt. He was in love with this little creature. It was as wonderful, nearly, as to be in love with a woman. The same joy overwhelmed him, the same baffling sense of nascent illness. He knew this kitten had entered his life not as a creature to be kept but as a being in her own right, significant and profound. He knew she knew he wasn't an outcast or a ghost but a deeply feeling man. His body may have been taken by the morgue, he thought, but his soul had remained unfettered. Together, they were free.

A corpse was delivered to him, the body of a professor from Teacher's College. He had died of coal-gas poisoning, the intake form said. Qing Yuan cleaned the body, wrapped it in a sheet, gave it to its cabinet. He returned to the workstation and looked at the form that had accompanied the dead professor. The words "Teacher's College" and "Victory Avenue" stabbed his eyes, and all at once he was choking on the stench of #19.

He had promised to uncover the truth about her death. He had exhausted himself struggling to scrape up the smallest clue. Then he'd been arrested and tortured, and then Lao Jia had been arrested and tortured and killed, and then he'd been made into an outlaw, a walking breathing dead man, and then he'd been taken and tortured—again.

He hadn't wanted to give up on #19. She would know this if she could. He had been faithful. He was faithful, still, tethered to her by reasons he could never speak, haunted, in fact, by the incomprehensibility of it all. And Feng Ge's husband, he thought— the man had been killed under mysterious circumstances, as well, on the same day, no less, as had been #19. It could have been mere coincidence, Qing Yuan knew, though he'd never believed that. Everywhere there were liars and sycophants and informants and crooks. He had seen them, hundreds of them, along with the countless others, and suffered at their monstrous hands.

He scratched Xi'er between the ears and kissed her. "Just for a few minutes," he said, and closed the door against her protests. He went to the shift manager's office and told the woman there he had to leave for a family emergency.

"But you don't have a family," the woman said. Qing Yuan stood before her, willing her to submit. "I'll send a cleaner," she said at last.

He took Xi'er from the cabinet and placed her in her bag and got on his bicycle and rode into the dark, the air as thick as velvet. He rode down the broken streets beneath pale streetlamps and the shadows they cast. A light breeze mounted, the first he could remember in weeks. The sound of rustling leaves filled him with nostalgia for a time he felt he'd never lived. In the distance a horn blew out, mournful as a human cry, the rumble of a train shaking the city's foundations. He passed prowling drifters, a lone woman in a circle of yellow light with her hands on her knees, coughing.

Xi'er remained quiet in her bag. Qing Yuan knew she could hear him. "This woman," he said. "They sent her to me months ago. She was slaughtered, and I never knew why, but I still want to know."

He turned into Victory Avenue, headed toward Teacher's College. The gate had been secured with an enormous padlock. He leaned his bicycle against a wall and sat in the dirt with Xi'er in her bag. He stretched his legs before him, unzipped the bag, and slipped his hand inside to stroke the kitten.

A long while passed before the silhouette of a streetsweeper appeared at the end of the street. The man was pulling a cart. He set it down and retrieved an oversized broom and began to sweep in practiced rhythmic strokes. Every few meters, he'd stop to drag the cart forward and fill it with the rubbish he'd gathered. Then he'd take up the broom and start again. The scrape of the bristle over the concrete and stone was hypnotic.

Qing Yuan patted Xi'er and zipped the bag and hung it on his handlebars, then leaned against a young tree to smoke. The man saw Qing Yuan but turned back to retrieve his cart and collect another pile. Finally he raised an arm to his sweaty face and said hello.

"Want one?" Qing Yuan said, and offered the man a cigarette.

The man looked at the street as if calculating whether he'd worked long enough to warrant a break. "Why not?" he said. They squatted to the curb and smoked in silence. "Do you work here?" the man said, nodding at the padlocked gate.

"I work in the hospital," Qing Yuan said, and pointed. "The one over there."

"I know where it is," the man said.

"How long have you been doing this?"

"I've swept this very street more than five thousand times." The man was enjoying his cigarette. It was as if he'd freshly acquired the habit and was still reveling in its secrets. "It's hard to believe now that I think about it. Sixteen years I've been doing this."

"I clean the corpses," Qing Yuan said. "But guess what? I've been doing it for sixteen years, as well." He snubbed his cigarette beneath his toe. "The only difference is that I've lost count."

The man chuckled. "More or less we're in the same herd."

Qing Yuan lit another cigarette for both of them. They sat in the mossy warmth, easy in the silence.

"They sent me a naked woman a few months back," Qing Yuan said. "She had been butchered. I've seen thousands of dead bodies, but never anything like that." The man looked into the night from behind his smoke. "Someone told me she had been picked up somewhere in this vicinity."

The man turned to Qing Yuan and looked into his face. "What do you want to know?"

"I just wish I could forget what I've seen."

The man squeezed his cigarette behind the ember then rolled it to-and-fro until the ember fell away. He tucked the remains into his breast pocket and sighed. "I wish the same," he said, to Qing Yuan's surprise. All over his body his hair stood up. The moon seemed to have doubled in size. Qing Yuan could see what he hadn't the moment before, an empty can of peaches across the street, a broken shoe in front of a heavy roll-up door.

"I heard the pleading, the crying," the man said. "There was terrible grunting and laughing. It was just sounds, bad sounds, I'll admit. Anyone who heard them would've known it wasn't the sound of a party. I dropped my broom and snuck over as fast as I could, but by the time I'd got there—here in this very spot, as a matter of fact—there was nothing anyone could do." The man fretted at his thighs and shook his head. "I couldn't believe she was still breathing. It was the most horrible thing I've ever seen."

Relief washed through Qing Yuan. All this time he had known it was here that #19 had met her terrible fate even as he had endured his doubt in a vacuum of shameful, willful secrecy. Someone had known what had happened. This man was him. Yet he, as would have anyone in his place, had said and done nothing, not because it hadn't mattered to him, but because to have done so would have jeopardized his own fragile grasp on existence. The man had known nothing could come of his knowledge past his own suffering. Had he interfered, Qing Yuan knew, had he but spoken of the matter to anyone with the power to do something about it, another man would be sweeping the streets in his stead.

He ached for the man. He, too, had to move through the rest of his days with the proof in his mind, a single heinous image, of the depths his fellows could plumb. Nothing he or Qing Yuan said would change anything. #19 would never be avenged, much less bask in the weakest ray of justice. Neither he nor this man could escape what they had seen. They would always know. It was a terrible thing to be bonded by tragedy. It was as much a relief to this man, Qing Yuan guessed, as it was to himself to have found a comrade in pain. He might never see this man again, yet neither of the two would forget this moment.

Dawn was near. The breeze had picked up. The night had cooled. Qing Yuan was no longer sweating. "I live in Worker Village," he said. "It may be a coincidence, I don't know, but my neighbor's husband was killed the same night. I've never been able to get it from my head that the two are somehow related."

"I can't speak to that," the man said, and took the half-smoked cigarette from his pocket.

"No need for that," Qing Yuan said. He tapped a cigarette from its package. "Here."

The man waved him off. "I like the flavor of an old cigarette," he said. "It reminds me of my childhood." Qing Yuan lit the man's stub and then his own cigarette. "There were three of them," the man said. "But like I told you, I don't know anything about a fight. I only heard her screaming. I hadn't got here yet before they took off on their tricycle. Someone else was lying on the bed between two of them, though. I won't forget that, either. Their legs were dangling from the back as they rode away. More than that it was too dark to tell."

The city had begun to rouse. Faint hues of pink and lavender brushed the sky. The first buses of the day grinded in the distance.

The man stood up. "Back to work," he said, and ambled to his broom.

"You're a good man," Qing Yuan called out.

24.

He sensed it before he heard it. He paused, his rag over the face of the corpse with which he was almost finished, and held his breath. The earth seemed to tremble, though he couldn't trust himself to say it wasn't another of the illusions that had taunted him since his release from the coal room and his subsequent beating at the struggle session. He thought to ask the face, once plainly quite handsome, whether it had noticed a change in things, but then the indisputable rumble of a big truck sounded from the street, growing louder as it neared.

The clanging of equipment, the clattering of metal and wood, the shouting and snorting of obnoxious men, the groan of the truck's hydraulic lift that soon followed brought to mind the recent announcement that an assembly hall for struggle sessions would shortly be built next to the morgue. Until today that had been no more than a possibility. Now that it was real, Qing Yuan understood, the relative peace he'd come to find here with Xi'er was sure to be spoiled.

He put the corpse away and went to the toilet. He scrubbed his hands then plunged his head into the water and stayed until his head had cleared. The ruckus outside hadn't abated. A man coughed a number of times then cleared his throat and spat. Tools clanked. Another man shouted. Finally, the truck revved up and chugged away.

Xi'er had retreated to the back of her cabinet, her eyes wide and ears against her head. He scooped her up and sat in his chair and ran his hand along her back, and soon she began to purr. Everything was as it should be, he thought, for now, anyway. But within moments, the shriek of a woman startled him and Xi'er both.

"Glory to the Revolution!" the woman cried. "Glory to the cement!"

Qing Yuan returned Xi'er to her cabinet and secured the door. Outside, the moon was close to full. Everything beneath it shimmered with silvery perfection. He walked around the corner of the building toward the sound of the voice, which, as he'd presumed, was where the earlier disturbance had come from.

Sure enough, the woman stood tottering where he thought she would, waving a shovel as she ranted about revolutions and cement. She was disturbingly thin, her face beneath her frayed straw hat closer to an open rictus than a medium of complex expression.

She was familiar to Qing Yuan, he knew he'd seen or met her, and yet he couldn't say where. Then it struck him—this creature was the gynecologist with whom he'd spent those terrible days in the coal room. Her clothes hung about her tattered and filthy—filthier, even, he thought, than Fan Fan's so-called clothes. She had wrapped her ankles with rough twine around an oversized pair of broken rubber galoshes. From a rope about her waist hung a bag as tattered as the rest. He looked at her face again. It was hard not to. The hollowed cheeks, the sunken eyes, the whole of this face in the silvery light was as gray as the faces of the dead he cleaned every night of the week. The gynecologist had been driven insane.

Qing Yuan started toward her and waved. "Hello!" he said.

"I'm working," she said as though she were terrified. "I've never stopped. Can't you see?" She stabbed at the earth with her shovel. "Who are you?" she said.

"It's me, the morgue keeper. We sat next to each other in the coal room." She shuffled closer, squinting at his face. "Remember?"

"You're the one who sleeps with the corpses," she said, and laughed. "What did you say you call yourself?"

"The morgue keeper," Qing Yuan said. "And you're the gynecologist."

"No!" she said. "I am a cement mother!" She stepped to the pile of powdery cement the workers had left behind and began to shovel the stuff one place to the next. "I mix the cement, a truckload a day, every day. I work with the construction boys, but it's always the mother who gets fucked." She turned to Qing Yuan scowling with her terrible face. He realized that her hair had not grown back after the Red Guards had shorn it away. "I build your roads, I build your houses, brick by brick, I build them all. I mix the cement with my blood—yes, my blood, my beautiful delicious blood!"

Qing Yuan never had more than his cigarettes to offer anyone. He would have given this woman the clothes off his back had he had more to replace them. He shook a cigarette from his pack and extended it.

The gynecologist threw down her shovel and wiped her eyes with the heel of a hand. Qing Yuan lit both their cigarettes, and they smoked in the silvery light.

"The rats sleep with me, you know, but they eat better. Their little teeth can gnaw the bones." She opened her mouth wide and pointed to it. "I can't even *think* about bones. All my teeth are loose."

Qing Yuan couldn't see that her teeth were loose, though it was impossible to overlook how many of them were missing. In all probability they were the very teeth the Red Guards had knocked from her mouth that awful day in the corridor outside the coal room.

"I've got some crackers in my drawer, if you—"

"I'm not hungry anymore. I *was* hungry, for days, for weeks. A hand—a concrete hand—wriggled into my vagina and pulled my intestines out. That happened every day, for weeks, if you can believe it." She jabbed the cigarette between her lips and held her stomach. "Do you know this concrete hand even has a name?" Qing Yuan gawked at this poor woman, sickened for her and her circumstances. She flicked her cigarette away and tugged at his shoulder. "It's called hunger," she whispered. "But it's okay now. Those days are gone. I just ate two legs."

"I'm sorry?"

"Two *baby* legs," the gynecologist said, and pointed toward the entrance to the hospital, "grilled on the fire. I smelled the meat and snatched up the baby and ate its legs." She began to weep while thrusting her fist in the air.

"I am so very sorry," he said. She needed help, but no one could deliver it. "I have to go," he told her. "I'm still working. But I'll come back, if you stay here." He gave her his package of cigarettes. She shoved them into her filthy bag and pushed back her hat to scratch her ravaged head. "Please," he said, "tell me your name? I never knew."

"I am the cement mother," the gynecologist said and began to cackle. "Didn't I just say that? I'm the baby-eating cement mother!"

This area outside the hospital hadn't been a garden, yet the day before it had been green, more or less. Where there had once been grass and shrubs now lay a plot of dirt and concrete and equipment and wood, all of it for a structure to host the prosecutions of his fellow citizens, the way, he thought, he himself had been prosecuted not too long ago.

He ached around the clock. His eyes had turned yellow. His wounds and sores wouldn't heal. He had begun to cough. He reviewed his condition as he picked his way back to the morgue and concluded that he was a mess. And yet next to the gynecologist, he thought, some would say he was lucky. He was not the body waiting for him in the morgue. He was not the gynecologist.

No one had delivered a corpse in his absence. His gratitude had been reduced to small blessings such as this. Mostly, though, now, he gave his heart to Xi'er. She had been patient. He listened for her as he walked toward the workstation. Already she had learned to make no sound in his absence, though neither he nor his fellows had taught her.

He entered the room and tsked, and she began to meow with joy. He brought her to the chair. He stroked her back. He murmured with his nonsense words. He was not alone anymore, and neither was Xi'er. No one had suspected it, no one had imagined it possible, but this little creature had transformed a place of morbidity and despair into something approaching a home with a loving family. He wished Lao Jia were here. However rough his old friend had been, Xi'er, he knew, would have melted his cynical heart.

Near 5 a.m., Qi Chu rushed in, a very different man. "Please!" he said. "I beg you to cover my shift! I need to go home now!"

The kitten hopped off Qing Yuan's lap and sniffed at his colleague's shoes. Then she sat on the floor, her eyes as calm as they were alert. Another time, Qi Chu would have scooped her up with glee. In this moment, in the grip of full panic, he didn't even see her.

"What is it?" Qing Yuan said.

"My wife was reprimanded for something she didn't do, then got into a fight with the Party Secretary. Then she went home and took rat poison. My daughter found her on the floor. She's in the hospital as we speak!"

"Do you know if she's going to make it?"

"Qing Yuan, I don't know anything more than that she's in a coma, and that I must go immediately!"

"Go, then—just go!"

"Please," Qi Chu said, "I would never do this. You know I wouldn't, but could you please lend this poor bastard a couple of cents?"

Qing Yuan hand him a five-yuan note. "Is this enough?"

"Thank you!" Qi Chu said, and rushed away.

Xi'er circled Qing Yuan's legs, pausing now and then to press against them. Within seconds she was purring. He scratched her between the ears.

"I have to finish cleaning," he said, and went into the corridor.

A sharp pain stabbed his belly. He retched over the toilet. Nothing came up but a dribble of bile. Nausea surged through him, each wave more intense than the last. It couldn't be food poisoning. He had eaten almost nothing for two days. He ran the water over his head for several minutes, trying to regain himself as the explosions pounded his temples. He dried his face and head and returned to the workstation. Xi'er lay sprawled on the chair. He brought her to his lap, and as ever she began to purr.

He struggled to complete the paperwork needed to transfer several corpses to the crematorium. By the time he'd finished helping the cleaner with the bodies, he had no strength to stand. The pain had been unrelenting. "I'll only be a minute," he said to Xi'er, and placed her in the cabinet.

He registered at the outpatient department and was seen within thirty minutes. The pharmacy, however, was unattended. He waited until a woman appeared at the window. He gave her his name and received a bag of pills, three of which he swallowed dry.

Already he'd taken too long away from the morgue. Who knew how many bodies would be waiting for him, he thought. And what if someone had reported his absence? He had no water-tight explanation. Illness, even severe illness, no longer sufficed to exempt anyone from their duties. He hurried through the lobby, his head down, still aching, still sweating.

He looked up to maintain his bearings and saw Feng Ge, not ten feet away, with her daughter. The girl must have been suffering badly for Feng Ge to have brought her here this early. The girl didn't notice Qing Yuan, but rushed toward the fish tank that had enamored her before.

Feng Ge looked into his eyes. The kindness in them confused him. At the struggle session she had refused to acknowledge his existence. Now she watched him as he passed. He could feel her gaze, yet he kept on. This would be the last time he'd see her, he believed, or rather, he thought, never again would she acknowledge him as she just had. He hurt too much to feel, to consider the meaning of his feelings. He had to work. That was all. Then he heard her call his name.

He stopped and turned. He hadn't been mistaken. Her eyes, he was sure, glimmered with sorrow. "I'm sorry," she said. "I'm sorry for everything that's happened."

An announcement blared from the loudspeakers at each end of the lobby. "Attention please!" a woman's hard voice said. "The canteen is closed today. No food will be served." He looked up to see Feng Ge, to tell her he understood, but she was gone.

A body lay on a gurney in the corridor. He freed Xi'er from her cabinet and shut the workstation door. He wheeled the corpse into the morgue and began to clean it. The woman had died of "cerebral hemorrhage," the intake form explained. Finished, he swung the gurney about and saw cabinet #19. He should have told Feng Ge what he'd learned from the streetsweeper, he thought. She deserved to know the truth about her husband's death. Or perhaps she didn't. Sometimes, he reflected, it's better to remain in the dark, not for the sake of the dark, but because it was kinder than the light.

By noon Qing Yuan felt much better. Xi'er had livened up, as well. The little thing was bouncing around, swatting at the pom-pom Kong Jiu had brought her, attacking Qing Yuan's shoelaces.

"Calm down, now," he said, and ran his hand along her back.

A sensation coursed through him that at first he didn't recognize. He had to think about it for a time before understanding that it was simple hunger. He put Xi'er in her bag and taped a note on the door explaining he was taking lunch.

The crew of men building the new struggle session hall had been yacking and banging throughout the day. Now it was quiet, too quiet even for men on a break. As he had suspected, not only had the men stopped working, but most of them had crowded around a mountain of cement. Try as he might to peer through the men, he couldn't see the object that had drawn them. He pushed through the crowd to find a twisted body flat out in a puddle, its bald head and sunken face smeared with filth. A dirty straw hat lay cockeyed on a pile of bricks a few feet off. He looked at the body again. It was the gynecologist.

Qing Yuan placed his fingers under her nostrils and felt the warmth of her breath. He spoke to her. Her eyes fluttered for a moment. When she opened them and saw Qing Yuan, he put a hand beneath her head and drew her up.

Behind them, a man began to shout. "Enough fun now, lads. Get your asses back to work!"

A grizzled bare-chested man set a tin of cornbread and watery soup next to Qing Yuan. "Maybe this will help," he said.

Qing Yuan lifted the tin to the gynecologist. She sipped a little then shook her head. One of her eyes had shut and the other looked at him half-open. "I'm not really hungry," she said.

"But you have to eat," he said. "Let's move you out of the way, someplace where you can rest, and I'll go get you some lunch." He set the bag with Xi'er in the shade against a wall then helped the gynecologist.

Unless he was at the morgue, where he kept Xi'er in the workstation, wherever he went, she went, too. He took her bag and rushed off to a nearby eatery. He ordered two bowls of fried rice then waited at a table near the door for his number to be called, Xi'er between his feet.

The naked lightbulbs overhead flattened everything in the windowless space. For a moment, Qing Yuan felt he'd been transported to a two-dimensional world. The woman a few tables off looked like a cutout figure in a window display. A massive young man with three plates of food before him could have been the drawing of a child.

All summer long the heat had refused to give. Though the days had somewhat cooled, still, here in the eatery, it was sweltering. The air hung thick with the smell of hot food and the smoke of coal. Flies menaced everything, the people, the food, the grease on the walls, anything that hadn't been recently cleaned. Tramps shuffled table to table with no one to keep them from the customers. They held out their tins as they stared at the food, drooling as they mumbled. "Mercy!" they said. "Mercy!"

The man who'd been dispensing the meals appeared in the pick-up window and called Qing Yuan's number. He pushed his way to the counter and showed the man his ticket. He slid two bowls of fried rice to Qing Yuan, who walked them back to his table. He set down the bowls and knew right away that something was wrong. His body felt as if it had been sucked clean of everything in it. He looked to the floor beneath the table. The bag with his kitten was gone. Xi'er was gone.

He got down on his knees and searched among the legs under the tables. He couldn't see a single bag. Someone had taken his, he knew. Someone had stolen his kitten. A pair of tramps loomed over his rice on the table when he stood up, mumbling their incessant pleas.

"My bag!" he said, knowing it was useless. "Have you seen my bag?" The tramps looked at him as though he were only mouthing the words.

He rushed into the street, wild with panic. Behind storage sheds, in and around piles of wood and coal, behind trash bins, under carts and trucks, in stairwells, alcoves, doorways, and nooks, up and down the way, everywhere he looked, calling Xi'er's name, tsk-tsk-tsking, he saw just wood and coal and carts and the random trucks, nothingness, nothingness—his little Xi'er was gone. He scanned up and down the street again and again, calling her name, meowing at times, once he'd checked that no one could hear him. She would come to him, he knew, if she were there.

He looked up to the windows of the two-story buildings, hoping she might have escaped her captors and flown to a ledge outside a window. From the gutter around the eatery's roof dangled what looked like the handle of his bag. A ladder leaned against the wall. He steadied it and without pause began to climb. The rotting wood groaned under his weight, rung by rung, but he reached the top and stepped onto the roof.

He saw the bag. It was his but empty. He sniffed inside. It smelled wonderfully of Xi'er. She couldn't be far, he thought, unless someone had stolen her to sell to the zoo or, worse, to eat themselves. But he hadn't the strength to think that far. The thought itself, distant as he strove to keep it, weakened him with despair. She *had* to have escaped, he kept telling himself, she *had* to have been hiding, waiting for him to find her, waiting to be saved.

It had been a long time since the roof had been cared for. Weeds had sprouted along the edges of the tar paper. Broken glass glittered in the full sun—from bottles smashed by drunks, he guessed. Whole bricks were missing from the chimney, its mortar crumbling away. He tiptoed about whispering Xi'er's name, tsking and tsking, all in vain. In his head he begged her to come back. *You can't leave me like this*, he thought. *You can't leave me to myself.*

A sudden rage surged through him. He felt like a father whose patience has worn thin. *Stop playing hide-and-seek with me, you little devil! Wherever you are, just come out!* And then he caught himself, and lapsed into remorse. *Forgive me, I didn't mean it. I'm just so worried. I'm just so scared. Please,* he thought, *if only you'll come back.*

He descended the ladder, glad, when the last rung broke, that he'd been cautious, and skittered through the streets. Everything— the houses, shacks, buildings, streets, windows, cars, buses, carts, lamp posts, people, trees—everything swirled at the periphery of his sight like through a dirty veil. The stench of #19 filled his head. He'd never be rid of her, he'd be forever haunted by the odor she'd become, an image without shape, an odor in the shape of a mutilated woman, it made no difference, he couldn't distinguish one from the other anymore. He was as helpless as he'd been in the dark of the coal room, waiting to be sentenced.

The pain in his belly set in again, and then the waves of nausea. He stopped cold, wheezing, flailing in search of a post or a wall to steady him. He wanted to cry out for help, but when he opened his mouth, he was abandoned by his voice. He pictured Xi'er alone and frightened in this city of the dead, wandering aimlessly, as did everyone now that the Revolution had strangled with its monstrous grip the little that had remained to them. The crowds were no longer crowds but incorporeal shrouds, he thought, such an ugly rhyme, he thought, though there was no other way to put it. This was the forsaken truth. His happy little girl knew nothing of this place. He had protected her from it, the ugliness this world had become. She had no way to know which way was home.

His knees began to ache, and while the heat had been no less ferocious than in the many days before, his feet felt as cold as if he'd been standing on a lake of ice. He thought he heard Xi'er cry, her sweet meow calling out from the depths of a pit or perhaps from inside the crumbling chimney on the roof. He didn't know whether to dig or to climb. He couldn't will himself to move. He wasn't him any longer, he realized, he had nothing left to will or to move.

Until this moment, despite the catalogue of adversities he'd weathered, he had remained a loving man. He hadn't lost who he was. His dignity had preserved him. His compassion for the world and all that it held had given him the strength to continue on. He hadn't descended with the rest, he had not collapsed. He had, in short, remained himself.

Now these, too, his virtues and his frailties, along with anything else he'd known, had abandoned him. He was merely Qing Yuan, now, a name without a person, he thought, like a suit without a body.

Where was his happy girl, the innocent creature emerged like a gift from a basket beneath the bed of his tender aunt? Sister Wang had known from the start, he thought with regret. Salvation and doom were one and the same. She had never judged him, as he had believed since the day she'd announced the burden he carried in his face. *He* had judged *her*. She had but warned him, lovingly, a very different thing, about the hardships to come. Then, in the guise of a supplicant begging for a few bits of wood, she had led him to the means of his salvation.

What would she say to him here on this desolate street? How with her bounty of wisdom could she make sense of something so plainly insensible? In the dark of the blazing day, he called out for Xi'er. Meow, he cooed, meow, meow.

25.

AT THE END OF a gravel path loomed an abandoned church. Dusty spiderwebs gleamed from the soffits in the crumpling portico. Wasps bounced around a number of enormous hives. He sat on the porch and lit a cigarette.

A woman with a baby shambled his way on a gimpy leg. The child, swaddled in rags, had been crying since he first saw the two approaching. It wanted to be held, or it was hungry or sleepy or in pain or discomfort after having soiled itself.

Qing Yuan's mother had once told him that babies cried for these four reasons alone. If treating the first didn't work, she had told him, one needed merely to go through the list. "They are so simple," his mother had said, "babies. My mother taught me this when we had you, and you were no different. Though I must say you rarely cried, and then not so much."

The woman paused to lean on a forked stick. To see her struggle as she glared at the dented tin in her hand, the thing must have weighed like a mountain. She pressed it against her leg to keep it from slipping away. Her strength, he thought, could be no more than a phantom that stayed with her to hear a pathetic song.

Like the thousands of others of her kind, anonymous and dispossessed—Fan Fan, he thought, the gynecologist, the poor zombies in the eatery that had robbed him of his happy kitten, the endless shuffling hordes that clogged the walks of just about every sector of the city—this woman's destitution and filth preceded her. She wore no clothes worth mentioning. It was her shoes that Qing Yuan had fixed on. Despite the hemp with which she'd bound them, the caps were in shreds, so that her toes, blackened and gnarled, wagged nakedly about. She had nothing but her baby, this was plain, and nothing to hide or lose.

She had seen Qing Yuan but to his surprise said nothing. He hadn't expected a greeting. No one but Fan Fan had said hello to him or bid him a good day. Always it was a plea. But he understood. This woman and her child had indisputable need. Her living was her begging. She would get nothing without the labor of her asking, he knew, which was why it confused him that she'd said nothing at all. Her silence touched him. He couldn't say why she'd not begged. It had something to do with respect, he believed. She had come upon a man alone on the steps of a church. Were it any place else, he had no doubt she'd have latched onto him straightaway.

She set her things on the ground and untied the baby from her back and slid down the trunk of an ancient poplar tree. "Okay, okay," she said to the child. "Please, won't you just stop for while?" The child was neither wailing nor sobbing. Qing Yuan presumed that, like its mother, it had no strength to do more than softly cry. The woman pulled up a few layers of clothes and offered the child her breast in a cupped hand. As soon as the baby had latched on to it and begun to suckle, its crying ceased.

She peeled open the tin and with a spoon from her sack scooped a gray blob into her mouth and began to chew with unexpected vigor. She knew she had no milk for the child. The boy dropped her breast and began to cry. She brought his mouth to hers and fed him what she had just softened.

After the child had swallowed a few times, it began to choke. The woman patted his back and shook his head until he burst out crying again. "Forgive me, my dear boy," she cooed. "Such a sensitive boy, I understand! I feel your pain, believe me, I do. Shh,

shh, my little one, cry as you like." She went on this way, but the baby wouldn't stop. "The only thing to ease your pain," she said, "is sleep. Try to sleep, please?"

Qing Yuan rose and dusted himself down. He walked to the woman and handed her a two-yuan bill. It was a colossal sum, they both knew. The woman gawked. Her rotten teeth stuck out from her half-filled mouth. She was smiling, Qing Yuan supposed, or trying her best. She shoved the bill into her clothes as she babbled her thanks. He could feel her staring as he made off. The money he had given her, if she spent it on food, would keep the two from starving for another few weeks.

Near the hospital he passed through a quarter of shabby little houses crammed together like a child's painted blocks. He peered into the gloom of an alley filled with household junk. As his eyes adjusted, he made out a pod of tattered men squatting along the walls, their faces like wilted cabbage.

Down the way he saw an old man with a matted beard, bald but for some long grey hairs at the back of his neck. Qing Yuan thought at first that the man was sleeping, but the moment he paused, the man looked up to survey him.

"Do you live here?" he said with gruff authority.

"I work in the hospital over there," Qing Yuan said, and nodded.

"A doctor then." A preschool boy skittered past with a crooked stick. "Tell your grandma to bring me some water." The boy nodded at the old man and ran along. "That damn stupid woman puts too much salt in my food. It won't be long, I'm sure, till I die from salt poisoning."

"I've never heard of such a thing," Qing Yuan said.

"And you call yourself a doctor." The codger glared at him like he might at someone who'd slapped his face. "They use salt to poison cats and dogs all the time." Qing Yuan stiffened at the thought of poisoning cats. The old man sensed his alarm but continued on. "There was a Korean guy down there," he said, and gestured to the alley Qing Yuan had just passed, "who ate dog meat whenever he could get his hands on it. He used to go into the countryside during the winter to steal the peasants' dogs. His secret trick, he told us, was the salt. And when he couldn't get a dog he'd take a cat." The old man smiled at the memory. He nodded with great vigor as he spoke. "You can't imagine how good this place smelled when he cooked them in the alley!"

"Speaking of cats," Qing Yuan said, "maybe you've seen a kitten around here?"

"Today?"

"She's pretty small," Qing Yuan said, shaping the kitten with his hands. "Like this."

"No cats here," the old man said with a grimace. "No pets. No animals. That's the goddamned law these days. I hear an owl hooting now and then, but I've never seen it. How about you?"

"I've never heard an owl, not one in this city my whole life."

"Well, all right, but I'm not yanking your chain. Come here at night and you'll see why the owls. No one owns a cat. It's the law, you see, but there are plenty of wild ones scampering about. That's why the owls."

Qing Yuan told the old man he was glad that at least the owls were keeping the city clear of feral cats, then said he had to be on his way.

The old man shouted in the direction the toddler had run off, demanding his glass of water. Then he closed his eyes and dropped his chin to his chest. He looked just as he had when Qing Yuan met him.

It wasn't until he'd neared the hospital that he remembered the gynecologist. He had promised to bring her food. Instead, he'd neglected her. She had been left alone for hours. He rushed to the construction site. She had disappeared.

26.

KONG JIU SAT HALF-DRUNK at the desk, his dinner pail before him. "Finally," he said when Qing Yuan opened the door. "The shift manager told me you'd left a note but never come back." Qing Yuan poured water from his thermos into a cup and took a seat. "I suppose you already know you're in serious shit."

A large bag was propped up in the corner. "What's that?" Qing Yuan said.

"My stuff. Bedroll, toothbrush, wash bowl, tin. Everything I need."

"I don't understand."

"I left my wife, goddamn it."

"But where are you going to stay?"

"I asked for a spot in the dormitory."

"That place is no better than a jail cell."

"All I need is a bed. And anyway, it'll give me more time to drink with you." Kong Jiu pinched a wad of cabbage and raised it to his mouth. Then he froze, his hand midair, the stuff falling from his chopsticks. He cast about the room, stupidly blinking, like a man who had forgot something critical but couldn't name. "Where's Xi'er?" he said.

"She ran away."

Kong Jiu's chopsticks clattered off his pail and to the floor. "No!"

"There was a woman at the construction site. She was in bad shape. I told her I'd get her some food. The canteen was closed, so I took Xi'er with me to the eatery down the way. I put the bag under the table and went to get the food. I couldn't have left her under my table for more than two minutes, but when I came back the bag was gone."

"Just two minutes?" Qing Yuan looked at the desk and sipped his water. It was far hotter than he thought it would be after hours in the thermos. It scalded his tongue, and he nearly dropped the cup. "Just because someone stole the bag," Kong Jiu said, "doesn't mean she ran away. I mean, whoever stole it might have killed her. She might already have been eaten—"

"She's *not* dead!" Qing Yuan slumped forward with his arms on his knees and clasped his hands. "She's *not*, all right? Don't say that again."

Kong Jiu lurched from his seat to pace in little circles as he scratched his tortured face. "Did you even *look* for her?"

"Where do you think I've been?"

"You put her in that stupid bag like she couldn't feel a thing. But she could—she *hated* that stupid bag." He struck a match and held it to Xi'er's cabinet while making the sounds he knew she loved. "She hated this thing, too," he said with disgust, and flung the match away. He opened and closed the door several times. "Goddamn Qi Chu. This was his idea," he said, and kicked the cabinet.

Qing Yuan put his face in his hands and rubbed his temples. Kong Jiu knew he'd gone too far. He took out his baijiu and filled two glasses. "Here," he said, and returned to his seat.

Qing Yuan swallowed the drink in a gulp and felt the liquor roar through his body. They sat like mutes, struggling to contain themselves until at last a door creaked open and the rattle of a gurney moved their way.

Kong Jiu looked homicidal. "A man can't even eat his dinner in peace!"

A cleaner peered through the glass then opened the door and placed his hands on his hips. "Well, isn't this just fine!" he said. "Drinking on the job!"

"Do I work for you?" Kong Jiu shouted.

"Whoa, whoa, whoa. I was joking!" The cleaner flipped a paper onto the desk. "This might be too much of an inconvenience, Comrade, but I'm afraid you'll have to sign on the dotted line." Kong Jiu scrawled his signature without looking and tossed back what remained of his drink. Seeing that neither Kong Jiu nor Qing Yuan was going to budge, the cleaner said, "The least you could do is move that damn thing off the gurney."

"Leave it," Kong Jiu said.

"Can't do that."

"Then come back for it, damn it!"

The cleaner moved off, grumbling behind his mask.

The corpse as usual had been covered, everything but its feet. One of them was colorless. The other was purple. Qing Yuan rose and wheeled the gurney into the morgue.

"Those feet," he said when he came back. "Right in my face."

Kong Jiu took an envelope of roasted peanuts from his drawer and poured half of them on the desk before Qing Yuan. "*Where did you look?*"

"Everywhere," Qing Yuan said, and refilled both their glasses.

One of Kong Jiu's peanuts fell to the floor. He picked it up and ate it. "Xi'er is smart. She was probably sick of being stuck with us ridiculous humans. Leaving was her way of sending a message."

Qing Yuan knew that Xi'er could sense things no human ever could. The first night he had brought her to the morgue, she'd lain across his desk while he filed his paperwork. Then, without any reason he could see, she leapt up as if from a nightmare and scratched his hand. He looked about, startled, and asked her what was wrong. She dropped to the floor and began to skitter about, her little tail switching. Qing Yuan tried to pick her up, but she wouldn't have it. Less than a minute later, a cleaner came in with a body. *This kitten knows when the dead are coming!* Qing Yuan had thought. He had heard of animals behaving oddly before an imminent earthquake or tsunami, but this sensitivity was of a different order. He took the body away, and when he returned, Xi'er was back on the desk, licking her paw and running it over her ear.

"This is where people quit," Kong Jiu said, and dropped another couple of peanuts. His hands were shaking badly.

"Speak Chinese," Qing Yuan said. "I have no idea what you're saying."

"This is where they quit living, quit being here, quit their endless struggle—fuck, I don't know. All I do know is that this goddamned morgue is the 'quit place.'" He flicked away his envelope of peanuts and kicked the cabinet again. "Xi'er sees how incompetent and hopeless we are. Can you blame her for not wanting anything to do with us?" Qing Yuan felt his friend's desolation but far from agreed with his reasoning. Xi'er loved him. She didn't care where she was, as long as they were together. She hadn't left. She wasn't sending some ludicrous message.

Kong Jiu rose and gathered his things. He looked like a man hanging from a cliff. "I'll catch the shift manager before he runs off," he said, "and tell him a story about what happened with you."

"Listen. If you can't find a place, you're welcome to stay with me till you get things figured out."

"I appreciate it," Kong Jiu said, and left.

Qing Yuan looked at the cleaner's form. "Suicide by jumping," it said.

He put on his smock and fetched a bowl of water and pulled back the sheet from the corpse. There before him, covered with blood and grime, lay the gynecologist.

Vertigo swept him away like a riptide. He collapsed to the floor and began to weep. "I'm so sorry!" he wailed. "I'm so sorry! I'm so very sorry!" The words wouldn't stop. Sadness, remorse, confusion, rage, despair—he had been consumed, he was flailing in slow motion at the bottom of an evil sea. He rolled to his side and curled up with his face in his hands, unable to stop the flow of words. "I'm sorry," he cried, "I'm sorry, I'm so very sorry, please, I am so sorry!" It seemed to him in his mad grief that if he said the words enough, in just the right way, as though they were a spell, the gynecologist would rise, and he would awaken beneath palm trees on white sands. He wept and apologized and wept and apologized, rocking uncontrollably, but nothing happened, nothing changed, the gynecologist was dead. He should have returned to her as he had promised. Had he returned, he knew, this would not have happened.

He wanted to flee. He wanted to leap from the highest tower. He wanted to drink a bottle of cyanide. He wanted no longer to exist. But the corpse of the gynecologist had taken him in her tiny phantom grip. He was bound to her now. He was bound to each and every corpse he'd ever cleaned, he realized, this was his doom—he'd never be free. He pulled himself up by the table and looked into the corpse's face, just as all those years ago Lao Jia had commanded he look into the face of the dead young man who'd been killed when his scaffolding had collapsed in the night.

"You were the strong one," Qing Yuan said. "You were the brave one. You were always true." He wiped the face with savage tenderness until every fleck of blood and grime were gone. "I'm sure your daughter and son will send you clothes, and socks and shoes, also. I'm sure they will come to honor you."

The dead woman's body had been broken in multiple places. She looked like a fossil from an archeology dig, like a woman who'd been smothered in a hail of lava and fumes then buried whole by an avalanche of earth, forgotten for millennia until some man with a spade tapped her ancient bones. He remembered the day they'd met. She had been terrified, but she had been whole. He remembered her in the dark of the coal room, chaste, still, clinging to a code of feminine poise from an etiquette book a hundred years old. All her life she'd been good through and through, unshakeable in her conviction and belief. She had been fragile like a woman, yet, like his mother, like his aunt, powerful, too, as only women ever are. She had spent her life giving life. The Red Guards would never break her, he had been sure. Yet here she was before him like the fossil of a hag. He had been, as he had too many times, very, very wrong. He could have saved her, he believed. He had wanted to save her. Unseen powers had forced his hand. Xi'er had been taken, and he had been taken with her, swooped away in panic and fear.

He washed the corpse like he'd never washed another, then covered her with the best sheet he could find. "I'll go to Gugu's if your family doesn't come. I'll get my mother's qipao and her best leather heels." He didn't have it in him to slide her into a cabinet. He was still in denial. She might get up yawning, as from a nap. He leaned against the cabinets, desolate and exhausted.

"They sent me a woman," he said, "at the beginning of the summer. She had been slaughtered. No one brought her clothes. I had believed that they would, that someone would, but no one ever did. She had been murdered and left in the dark on the curb. I should have dressed *her* in my mother's qipao. She deserved so much more, but I could have done that, at least."

Again he began to weep. After a long while he pulled down the gynecologist's sheet and bent to her face. "I will not let you leave here naked," he said. He covered her again and slid her into a cabinet but did not look at the number on the door.

27.

HE THRUST HIS HEAD under the water and let it course through his hair. He stayed there a very long time. In the workstation, as by habit, he looked about for Xi'er like the two were playing hide and seek. He felt inexcusably worthless and stupid.

Toward the end of his shift he began to sweep the corridor. A quarter of the way through, he paused to look at the *dazibao*. Lao Jia's name glared from most of them, as did his own. That the State had made each *dazibao* a different color seemed the height of perversion. Red, green, yellow, pink, orange, purple, blue—these were the colors of children's art paper, the color of paper dragons and cranes. To disguise their evil, and to appeal to our deepest emotions, the State had appropriated what had once been a thing of nostalgic delight and joy. He had turned his back on convention and taboo. He no longer cared that someone might hear him speaking aloud.

"Can't you sing something now," he said to Lao Jia's name on the *dazibao*, "just for me?" In vain he waited for Lao Jia's husky voice to burst out in jolly song. He moved along with his broom. "One summer day when we had tea together on our veranda," he said, "my mother told me that every year has its own color. 'It's not red or green or yellow or blue,' she said, 'but somewhere in between. And the color lives where everything lives, and where all of us live, and the color can remember.'" He leaned on the broom in front of another *dazibao* listing Lao Jia's many crimes. "That is wonderful," he heard Lao Jia say. "But what is the color of 1966?"

Qing Yuan left at six o'clock sharp. He had told a cleaner that Qi Chu wouldn't be coming in for his shift because his wife was in the hospital, and that he wasn't able to cover for him.

"You want me to pass the message to the shift manager, eh?" the cleaner said.

Qing Yuan walked into the early morning unsure where to go. The sky was opaque. A faint trail of pinkish light had appeared along the horizon. The air was damp and, as it seemed throughout the city, fraught with the smell of fumes and grease from the factories and bustling canteens. Smoke rose from the chimneys against the mounting sun. The city had begun to stir.

He tripped over a pothole onto his knees. The burns he'd sustained in the molten sand beneath the mockery of the Red Guard had never healed. He staggered to his feet. Nothing made sense. He was hollow. His bones had been purged of their marrow. His weakness was his strength because that was all he had. He had become one of the phantoms he'd lived among for years. Some dark hand had snatched away his spirit. He had been ground to dust. He looked at his ragged pants and broken shoes. It struck him that he'd never been so close to death.

The sun had risen without his knowing. The trees swayed in the breeze that had mounted. The summer had ended. The city swam before him, a liminal zone. Nothing was real. Nothing was unreal.

He bought an orange drink from a squalid corner store then sat in the dirt sipping from the bottle. Down the way coal smoke drifted from mud shanties and rusty tin shacks. Gray people passed him, lonesome and mean, glaring at him as if he were a tramp. Two naked boys maybe three or four years old appeared before him to stare in silence. Each of them held a rock.

"What do you want?"

They glanced at each other and held out their hands. Qing Yuan gave them each a coin, and they vanished around the corner.

Two women argued in the alley the boys had come from. One of the voices sounded familiar. He made his way to the corner and peered into the alley. Fan Fan lay on a torn straw mat with her legs stretched out, the bad one twisted, the other splinted with a board. A woman stood over her, shouting.

"For heaven's sake!" Fan Fan said when she saw Qing Yuan.

The other woman glared at him then picked up her water bucket and hobbled away. Fan Fan struggled to sit up. Qing Yuan approached, aghast. If not for her voice, he wouldn't have known who she was. She had always looked downtrodden, subhuman, in truth, filthy, injured, emaciated, weak. He'd thought it impossible for her to decline any further, and yet she somehow had. Her face hovered beneath him no more than a skull with yellowy eyes. The thinnest wisps of gray hair clung to her head like cobwebs. It was no exaggeration, he thought, to say she'd become death's shadow.

"What has happened, Fan Fan?"

The beggar smiled, the saddest expression Qing Yuan had ever seen. "Nothing, sir. I woke up with a broken leg." Qing Yuan squatted before her and extended a hand but stopped short of touching her. "You know it happened before. This time it's this leg," she said, and put her gnarled hands under her thigh as she coughed.

Qing Yuan looked into the woman's face, his heart racing with anger and despair. He couldn't understand. Nothing made sense. And yet the world went on.

"What are you doing in this neighborhood?" Fan Fan said.

"I lost my kitten," he said.

"That is terrible, sir! How ever will you find her in such a big city?"

It startled Qing Yuan that Fan Fan knew Xi'er was a girl. He remembered his talk with Fan Fan just after he'd received #19. He had intuited that she'd known more than she said. She'd spoken of "the missing woman" as if they might once have been friends. He had never pressed her, despite his suspicions. Fan Fan was crafty, he knew. Life had shaped her. She'd had to survive.

"I *will* find her," he said. He tapped a cigarette from his pack and put it between Fan Fan's lips. "This might help the pain," he said, and held up his lighted match.

She dragged at the cigarette breath after breath and for the first time since they'd met looked into Qing Yuan's eyes. "You've been nothing but good to me, sir," she said. The woman at the end of the alley had stripped naked on a bench to bathe herself with the water in her bucket. "By now you probably know as much as I do about that woman," she said.

That woman, Qing Yuan thought. The beggar had in fact known all along about #19.

"I'm sorry I didn't tell you sooner, sir. I was afraid. The night those Red Guards got her—" She gagged several times. It sounded like she was choking on a clump of hair. Her eyes filled with tears. Qing Yuan gave her his bottle of soda. She took it with desperation. Qing Yuan watched with heartache as her throat convulsed. "She wasn't a local," Fan Fan said at last. "I could hear her crying. Her accent, I couldn't tell where it was from."

At this, Fan Fan's old words sprang to Qing Yuan's mind. *She might not have a family in this city*, she had more or less said. "Her husband was there," Fan Fan went on, "Feng Ge's, I mean. He saw what was happening. He roared as he drove into them. But they knew what they were doing. Already they were covered with blood. Two of them had knives. He struggled with them. I couldn't see more than the bunch of them swinging and tussling. I could hear them shouting, too. And then he just fell."

Qing Yuan snubbed his cigarette in the gravel. The woman at the end of the alley must have known where the sun would shine. She was encircled by a corona of mellow light as she went on scrubbing herself with her rag. The boys he'd given money streaked past left to right. They looked like cartoons in a kaleidoscope. "And you?" he said.

Fan Fan twisted her head with a desperate cackle. "What do you think, sir?" she cried. "They would have killed me, too, had they got me. I hid behind a pile of garbage."

Qing Yuan touched her broken leg. He had never touched her before. It felt almost disrespectful, and yet as well the right thing to do. "They did this?"

"No one did it, sir," she said. The murderous Red Guards may not have been the culprits, but he knew she had been assaulted by someone she still feared. Her face, what remained of it, had in the strangest way turned in on itself, like the sea anemone in a book he'd read in high school. The badge with Mao Zedong's portrait glimmered from her chest. She drew at her cigarette and sighed. "It just happened," she said, "like everything else."

The woman flung the water from her bucket and patted herself down with another rag and wriggled into her clothes. Qing Yuan pressed a bill into Fan Fan's hand. He would not see her again, he knew. "Please, as soon as you're able, come to Worker Village."

"I most certainly will, sir," she said, and bobbed her head. "Thank you again. Thank you, sir, thank you."

Qing Yuan crossed through a construction site, peering here and there into the stands of weeds and piles of rubbish, tsk-tsking as he went in the hope Xi'er would hear him and manifest like a teensy djinn. He went on, refusing his defeat.

In a square at the center of an apartment complex, thousands of people had surrounded a green military truck. Between two bamboo poles at one of the openings to the square hung a great red banner announcing a "Public Execution Rally." He gripped a sapling next to a brick pony wall and stepped up to see a woman on a ladder with a megaphone. She was announcing the death sentence of five manacled people on the bed of the truck, four men and a woman on their knees, each attended by an armed Red Guard no older than sixteen or seventeen.

"These criminals are poison to our society," the woman with the megaphone shrieked.

"Kill them!" the mob seemed to cry as one. "Kill them all!"

At this distance, Qing Yuan struggled to make out the faces of the accused. Most of them had reconciled themselves to their fates and hunkered before the mob with bowed heads. One of them, however, looked up at the sky. Qing Yuan recognized him by his ruined face and thick white hair. It was the lab director. He was a murderer, the woman with the bullhorn shrieked, a man who had killed his own son. Nothing she was saying failed to delight the mob. They applauded and howled at her every word.

Qing Yuan felt invisible before this blood frenzy. He'd been transported back to some medieval gallows scene. The one thing missing were pitchforks and scythes jouncing above the mob. He stood transfixed, gripping the loose fabric of his trousers.

"To the firing squad!" the mob howled. "Kill them all, kill them now!"

Qing Yuan slipped from the low wall into the shrubs on its far side. He squatted to steady himself and vomited in the bushes. Mostly orange bile came up, he had eaten so little these last days. He stood hunched with his hands on his knees, heaving and sweating until the wave passed. He clambered back up the short wall then down to the walk on the other side. He fumbled through his pockets for his cigarettes then remembered he'd given his last to Fan Fan. Death was not a curse, he thought, the darkness was not a curse—emptiness was the curse, he thought, this void within him was the curse.

He stumbled past a row of metal and linoleum workshops. Broken glass glimmered among the leaves and tattered papers on the walk. He fixed on a shard three or four inches long and thought how easily it could kill a man. The pediatrician had known this well. Qing Yuan remembered the man's last peaceful smile when he'd set down his gruel and gone to the toilet whose window had been shattered.

He couldn't say how he'd reached it, but he found himself at the edge of the playground of a shuttered school. The gate was secured with a rusty padlock. He drifted down a cinder path, scouting the bushes and weeds. At the back of the school an open lot stretched out, filled with mounds of garbage. He picked his way through the clay pots and school chairs and hoses and buckets and nails, feces everywhere, the stench overwhelming—this was a toilet for the homeless—and yardsticks, pencil sharpeners, inner-tubes, lamps, pot and pans, destroyed mattresses and more.

Had he not been inured to the stench of the dead, he knew he wouldn't have had the fortitude to go on. He was nevertheless dizzy with anguish and its treacherous fellow, impotence. He sat on a block of concrete from whose sides jutted corroded rebar. The ache that had gnawed at him since his days in the coal room throbbed with increasing intensity. He put his face in his hands and groaned. Reason pranced in the distance, laughing. He had become the plaything of insanity.

In the silence, he could hear the flutter of a paper, the scratch of a bird. He thought at moments he could hear the earthworms crying. He sat listening until he heard a sound like the wheezing of some little being. He straightened up and cocked his head to concentrate. He heard the sound again, louder this time, and tiptoed toward the pile of rubbish he believed it was coming from. The sound went on, a creature was there, he knew, some animal in its death throes perhaps, panting out its final breaths.

He reached the pile but saw nothing more than a bicycle tire and rags and some shredded cardboard. He paused to listen and heard very well the same sound, the frail wheezing of a little being. He pushed away a stack of collapsed boxes and a moth-eaten coat. A beam of sun pierced the shadow. In its center lay Xi'er.

Both her ears had been torn and her fur choked with blood and grime. Vomit had crusted around her nostrils and mouth. She in no way looked like the kitten he'd fallen in love with, though he knew it was her. Those blue-brown eyes—jewels from heaven, he'd always felt—looked up at him with anticipation, sadness, and most of all, it seemed to Qing Yuan, relief.

He dropped to his knees and took her in his arms. "My girl, my girl, my girl!" he cried. "My happy little girl!" He dandled her and kissed her and ran his face across her ruined fur. The cut she'd had on her leg when he'd met her had been torn open and was infected. What else she may have suffered, he would fix. She was in his arms, like a teensy djinn.

Despite everything, she began to purr. She looked into his eyes the way she had since the day they met. It wasn't his eyes she saw, he knew, but his eternal essence, and he saw the same in hers. They two were a single jewel from heaven. He held her in the midst of this field of offal and trash and felt that the world's sins had been forgiven. No one could harm him ever again. Right and wrong had been made irrelevant. She put her tiny paws on his face. He believed she was smiling. She knew everything he didn't. She was a creature of pure essence.

Until now he hadn't known how he might navigate the world one moment to the next. Darkness and light had become indistinguishable. He had known no more than hardship and pain and, through that, understood how others might feel, as well. He had never been able to turn his back on the world. He had never wanted to, though he had tried. Now, he knew, he never would. He loved this kitten. This kitten loved him.

"We," he said to Xi'er, "are going to Gugu's to get my mother's qipao and heels, and after we give them to the woman who needs them, we are going home."

Xi'er meowed, not like a kitten, but like a cat. She licked his hand, what she'd never done before. He held her up to the sun and laughed.

ACKNOWLEDGEMENTS

I WANT TO EXPRESS my deepest gratitude to my editor, D. Foy, for his keen eye for detail, his thoughtful suggestions, and his unwavering support as we shepherded this book into the world. I do not exaggerate in the least how instrumental his guidance and expertise have been in shaping this work.

Thank you so much, D, for your dedication and, more importantly, for believing in me and my efforts. Nothing I say can truly express what a privilege it's been to work alongside someone who loves and understands the art of storytelling the way you do.

I also want to extend my heartfelt thanks to Leland Cheuk for his steadfast support and efforts, which have meant more to me than words can express.

ABOUT THE AUTHOR

Ruyan Meng left China after the Tiananmen Square Massacre to make her home in the United States. *The Morgue Keeper* is her debut novel.

7.13BOOKS